CHALLENGE ACCEPTED

WOLF APPEAL BOOK 2

KB ALAN

Second Shift Publishing

Editor: Kelli Collins

Cover Art by: Fantasia Frog Designs

❀ Created with Vellum

This book is dedicated to my parents. They taught me a love of books and encouraged me without hesitation in my writing, even when I explained about the smut (Someday I will write a book my dad can read, I promise). Everything good that I've done with my life, I credit to their unwavering love and support. Any mistakes I've made, they've given me the strength and wisdom to see through to the other side and turn to a positive. They are truly the best people that I know.

ABOUT THIS BOOK

Since being turned into a werewolf, Adam has been a loner. Practically a hermit. Okay, actually a hermit. When the local wolves and werewolves start experiencing weird behavior, he can't resist the pull to step up and see if he can help. And runs smack into trouble in the form of the werewolves' National President.

Myra's term as President is nearly over, but she's determined to track down the wolf who was attacked, and turned against his will. When she meets Adam, she only wants to help him live a full and happy life. Then she sees him naked. And gets to know him. And decides she wants a lot more for him than to just escape his lonely cabin in the woods.

To join KB Alan's newsletter and be informed of new releases, sign up at kbalan.com/newsletter!

CHAPTER ONE

The forest was his, and he no longer questioned it. Other wolves, natural wolves, roamed the same land, but they didn't bother him. They acknowledged his place in their territory and both sides were content to leave the other alone.

Adam paced the tree line to the north of his cabin, uneasy. Something was off in his territory and he needed to figure out what it was. He'd run across two seemingly rabid wolves, one the week before, the other just yesterday, that he'd had to put down. He'd felt sick doing it, but there'd been no choice. He couldn't risk the wolves making the others sick or getting too close to town. The farmers in the area already disliked the wolves, were pushing to have their protected status revoked and hunting season declared once again.

Adam had checked the werewolf database and forum—and wasn't it a kick in the pants that such a thing even existed—and managed to find out that the nearby werewolf pack, headquartered about thirty miles away, had also experienced something similar. Only, their incident hadn't been a natural wolf, but a sick werewolf who'd attacked its own pack members.

Adam shook himself in irritation, resettled his fur and headed back to the cabin. The information he'd seen online about the local pack's experience was sketchy. A young member had come out of the woods fighting, and it had taken a much stronger wolf than necessary to put her into submission. She'd finally gone unconscious, with a high fever, and when she woke, hardly remembered a thing. The worry, of course, other than not understanding what was making her and the natural wolves sick, was that if a stronger wolf were to be affected, they might cause real damage before someone powerful enough could stop them.

More worrisome was word from the town. There'd been talk about the rabid wolves, even though the local vet had stated that no rabies had been found. Talk about getting some hunters together to take care of the problem if the local officials weren't going to handle it. Adam wasn't sure which idea was worse, local hunters invading his land, firing willy-nilly, or the government coming in thinking they could do whatever it was government employees thought they should do to handle the situation.

He had to consider the possibility that the pack had more information than had been posted online, and if he didn't figure out what was going on, he was going to have to talk to them. Which irritated the hell out of him.

Pulling his human form to the front, he let the wolf fall away and strode into his cabin. He stepped into sweatpants and moved to the kitchen area.

A quick jiggle of his old teapot confirmed there was plenty of water in it and he turned on the stove. He pulled his not-so-old coffee press out of the cupboard and went through the mindless steps of producing coffee while he mulled over the problem. If the townspeople thought there was an outbreak of rabies, even though he was pretty sure that wasn't what was happening, they could go on the offensive. The last thing he needed was human hunters invading his property, firing at anything that looked like a wolf, including himself. Been there, done that, no need to repeat the experience, thank you very much.

When the coffee was ready, he moved to the couch and sipped thoughtfully. The first taste was perfect, and he smiled. He may live with very few of the trappings of civilization, but no way was he giving up good coffee.

Not getting shot again was also a priority, but so was keeping humans and werewolves out of his territory, just for his own peace of mind. Getting kidnapped, tortured and turned into a werewolf had been a bit more than his already somewhat introverted nature could stand, and he'd given up on wanting anything to do with people.

When he'd found and hacked into the werewolf site, he'd searched for stories like his, but come up blank. Apparently the crazy-as-fuck pack that had kidnapped, tortured and turned him had been the exception, not the rule.

Still, even after he'd come to that conclusion he hadn't been much interested in meeting up with others of his kind. He'd roamed the states for a couple of years until he'd hit on this part of Montana. Close enough to the pack that he could pretty much identify, and therefore avoid, where they lived and worked, but far enough away that he didn't have to work too hard to remain unknown.

He didn't remember a lot from that week six years ago. He recalled being invited out to a ranch by Paula Cage and enjoying a lovely barbecue before her crazy-ass brother had turned into a werewolf—an honest-to-god fucking werewolf!—and attacked him.

After that, things got hazy, though he still had uncomfortable flashes of Paula trying to get him to have sex with her while he was bleeding and only half-conscious. Fucking nuts, all of them. When the full moon had risen the next night, and he'd turned into a wolf himself, he'd taken off. Which was when the fuckers had shot him.

The whole thing still struck him as completely bizarre, even after all these years. He'd eventually come to realize that the pack he'd first encountered wasn't the norm, and he'd discovered there were plenty of werewolves out there who were normal, law-abiding citizens, but that didn't mean he had any desire to socialize with them, any more than he was willing to hang out with humans and risk being found out. Or risk hurting them; losing control somehow and turning them by mistake.

He finished his coffee and contemplated the teetering stack of books by the couch. It was almost time to make a trip into town, drop off the books he'd read, pick up some new ones, as well as other supplies. If he waited too long, it was a pain in the ass to haul the larger quantity of books to and from the old pickup he kept on the east side of his land. He divided up his trips, hitting the town that was closer to pack land only a couple of times a year, and interspersing that with trips to the other side of the mountain.

So far, he'd managed to avoid running into any of the pack while in town, and as far as he knew, they weren't aware he existed. He'd learned enough about their ways to figure he'd be able to talk himself clear of any situation, mostly due to the fact that he wasn't breaking any of their laws, other than remaining anonymous. Technically, he was supposed to let the Bitterroot hierarchy know he was there so they could make sure he was following said laws, but what they didn't know wouldn't hurt him. He'd been in the area three years with no contact and until now he'd seen no reason to change that.

With a sigh at the idea that it might finally be time to come out of the werewolf closet, he moved to turn on the generator, get some hot water going. He'd make dinner, run a load of laundry, wash the dishes, and take a nice hot shower before going to bed, sleeping on the problem.

Just before flipping the switch, he frowned at the distant buzzing sound coming from outside. It wasn't often he heard low-flying planes in the area, but it seemed like lately it had been more frequent.

He turned on the generator and grabbed a sweatshirt on his way to the front door, having cooled off from his earlier run.

The sun had set and the light was nearly gone, but he could just pick out the plane a couple of miles to the west, heading toward town. Something else to look into, he figured, though he wasn't sure where to start on that. Maybe he could hack into the local airport, see if it was possible to identify the plane that way. He made note of the time and went back inside to make his dinner. If he didn't have any brilliant ideas before morning, he was going to have to suck it up and do what needed to be done.

Two days later

The vast expanse of forest called to Myra, beautiful in twilight. She wished she could shuck her clothes, her shoes, those trappings of civilization that usually grounded her, stand naked in the cool mountain air for just a minute, before allowing the fur and simplicity of her wolf to overtake her. The wind whistled softly through the branches, birds called out cheerfully to each other, and the crisp, clean smells vouched for the two-hour drive out of the city.

Sighing, she turned her back on the enticing sight and faced the wolves who'd come out of the pack house to greet her.

She could feel their nervousness, should do something to calm their worries, but was too on edge herself. They'd called in to the National Council to report a problem but hadn't expected her, the current National President, to show up. What they didn't know was that their problem seemed to be coinciding with *her* problem, one she wanted to clear up as soon as possible. Needed to clear up.

Not that she could just fix it. That was the real tragedy. No matter what she did, what the pack did, there was no fixing this. An innocent man had been brutally attacked, turned into what he would surely perceive to be a monster, then escaped to live the life of a werewolf without the support of those like him.

If they'd found him, like she believed, she could offer that support now, answer any questions he might still have after all these years, let him know that the evil shits responsible for his attack had been taken care of. But she couldn't fix it. Couldn't give him back the life he'd lost.

The alpha pair gave her a slight bow and she nodded and managed a distracted smile before preceding them inside. She'd known Michael and Linda for years, but they weren't particularly friends. All reports she'd studied while flying north to meet them indicated that Bitterroot was a healthy pack, not very large considering the vastness of land available in Montana, but tight knit and happy.

They settled into seats and the pair waited for her to begin while Simone, the third in their pack hierarchy, brought in a plate of refreshments. Myra thanked her, accepted a cup of tea and took a sip, waiting for Michael and Linda to take their drinks as well.

"Linda," she began. "After you spoke to Tom about what had happened down here, he called me, as I may have a particular interest in part of your story. Would you mind going over what you told him, giving me the details directly?"

Tom, the current National Secretary and therefore main point of contact between the packs and the head organization, had called her as soon as he'd hung up with the Bitterroot alpha. He would have done that anyway, due to the problem the pack was having, but he'd also been excited to share the news about the unknown wolf.

"Of course. It started a few weeks back. One of the pack ran across a wolf that was acting sick. We thought rabies at the time. She had to put the poor thing down, and brought the body back." She glanced nervously at her husband.

"We considered destroying the body," Michael said, his back straightening.

Myra knew if he'd been in wolf form she'd see his hackles rising.

"But if there really was a rabies outbreak happening, the town needed to know."

She nodded her agreement and the couple's tension level eased down several notches.

"Animal control said they didn't actually find rabies, had some odd test results but couldn't say anything definitive," Linda continued. "He wouldn't confirm poison or drugs, said he needed to run more tests. We put the word out to the pack to be on the lookout for any other odd wolf behavior, and not to eat anything they weren't sure of, for fear of poison, but nothing happened for another week."

"Except," Michael jumped in, "the vet received another dead wolf, which he also confirmed was rabies-free."

"But we didn't know that at the time," Linda finished. "What happened next was one of our own wolves got sick. A few of the teens had gone out for a run, and this one, Denny, came back on his own, acting wildly out of control, completely unlike himself. Our first was able to subdue him until Michael showed up."

"He was sick, running a high fever, sweating, breathing hard." Michael stood and began to pace. "They said before Jake was able to calm him down he'd been attacking whoever came near, even our third." He gestured to where Simone had left the room. "Which is crazy, he's nowhere near strong enough to challenge a member of the hierarchy. Once I got there he was able to calm down even more and went to sleep for about twelve hours. When he woke up he barely remembered any of it, thought it had been a nightmare, or a fever-induced hallucination."

"Jake was the first to comment on the similarity to the sick wolf," Linda added.

Michael sat back down, took his mate's hand in his. "The next night, another of my wolves, a sixteen-year-old who I think will likely be hierarchy one day, turned up the same way. Out of her head, threatening anyone who came near. When I got there, I could tell that she was just barely hanging on to her control. Actually, once she realized I was there, she lost her control and attacked. We had to hold her down so I could force her submission. Once she submitted, it was just like it had been with Denny. Liv was sick, she slept, she barely remembers."

Shaken by the story, Myra considered. She'd never heard of such a thing. "Would you know if natural wolves up here were acting rabid?" Myra asked.

"Yes. No question. There are enough hunters, ranchers and

farmers in the area who hate that the wolves are protected. They would jump on any excuse to have that protection stopped. It's why we hesitated before going to animal control, but if there really had been an outbreak of something..."

Myra nodded. Some areas of the country had a much more delicate balance with the hunters and local population than others. "And then you met the lone wolf."

Michael glanced at his wife but she motioned for him to continue the story. "He showed up in town yesterday, walked up to one of our wolves and asked her for her alpha's phone number, or for her to call and give us his number. Linda and I went right out to meet him. Said his name was Adam and he lived not too far away."

"Wouldn't say where, exactly," Linda interjected.

"Wouldn't say where," Michael confirmed, "but said he had some acres and kept to himself, but he was concerned about the sick wolves. Said he'd heard we'd had a couple of sick kids, as well, and wanted to see if we had any new info to share."

"I'd like to know how he knew about the kids," Linda said, the anger in her voice clear. "It's not like it's something we were talking about freely."

"You guys didn't like him," Myra said.

Michael winced.

"He wasn't..." Now Linda hesitated. "He knew he was expected to let us know he was living here, he wasn't ignorant of the rules, he just didn't care. Blatantly."

Michael nodded. "But on the other hand, whether it seems like it right now or not, Linda and I, our hierarchy, we have a good handle on our region. We may not have known he was there, but we for sure would have known had he been making any trouble."

Linda pursed her lips. "I didn't like him, you're right. Doesn't sit well with me that he's out there all by himself, avoiding us for years. It's not natural. It's not wolf." She sighed. "But, I did believe him that he's been behaving himself, and that he's trying to help figure out this problem." She glanced at her husband, got a nod from him. "The other thing is, well...he's stronger than us. And it's *really* not natural for a wolf that alpha to not want to be pack. So, what's he doing out here, all by himself?"

Myra debated how much to tell the alpha pair. Ultimately, the matter couldn't be swept under the rug. Pretending it hadn't happened wouldn't make sure it never happened again. "I got a call a couple of weeks ago from Mountain Pack, in Northern Idaho. Seems their alpha found his mate, a woman named Hillary. She told him that she'd been attacked and turned, four years ago."

Linda gave off a gasp and Michael gaped at her.

"I know. It gets worse. An entire rogue pack had formed in Phoenix, Arizona. Led by a man named Ken Cage, who was related to the alpha pair in the Mesa Pack." She took a deep breath, trying to calm the anger that burned even now, weeks after bringing those wolves to justice. "Cage liked to find humans and convince his pack that they could be turned. Then attack them, and if they were female, which they mostly were, rape them, until they died."

Linda looked physically ill and Michael looked confused. "That doesn't make any sense, that's not how wolves are turned. Besides, anyone strong enough to live through that isn't going to stick around with the idiots who turned him."

"Exactly. So, not only was Cage a crazy bastard, he was also an idiot. And you're right, both wolves who survived escaped once they turned. The others didn't survive. To add insult to injury, the bastard couldn't even remember his other victim's name."

"And you think this Adam is this surviving wolf?" Linda asked.

"I hope he is. Cage says he shot the teacher that turned, but never found a body. Which doesn't mean he really got away, of course. But I'm hoping." If their Adam really was just a lone wolf, one who, for whatever reason, shirked the need for contact, companionship, and touch that most wolves craved, that was fine. But she needed to find her missing wolf, do whatever was possible to help him understand the world he'd been forced into, be as at peace as possible with the wolf within himself. Of course, there was always the chance that the teacher had died, but she would exhaust all possible efforts before giving up.

"That's just awful," Linda said. "To have lived all this time alone, no pack, no family, just..." She shook her head. Michael took her hand, his thumb gliding an absent pattern over her skin. For the first time in a long time, Myra felt a pang of longing for her mate. It had been more than fifteen years since Eric had been killed. Wolves touched a lot, so it wasn't like she didn't have physical contact on a regular basis, but it wasn't the same.

She shook her head and returned her attention to the couple. Wolves were pack animals. They needed to touch, smell, be with each other. The fact that Adam wanted nothing to do with them wasn't a good sign, but at least he'd come forward to help with the sick wolves. She focused on that.

"I know. I need to talk to him, find out if he's the same wolf. If he's not, I'll still help with the current situation while I continue to search for the teacher. If he is, I'm hoping we can figure something out to help him integrate, or adjust, or...whatever we can do." She paused, took a sip of her nearly forgotten tea. "He's stronger than you? Even as a pair?"

Michael nodded his confirmation. "Definitely."

"Then hopefully he really is the one I'm looking for. It would take a very strong wolf to survive what he did." She was anxious to meet him, to know for sure. "How did you leave it with him?"

"He gave me a cell phone number, took mine. Said he'd call if he found anything out, asked me to do the same. He was polite, didn't try and push any power or anything. I'm sure he knew we were irritated, but he stayed cool."

"I have no reason to believe that you don't have an excellent handle on this territory. If he'd been misbehaving in anyway, I'm sure it would have come to your attention before now."

They nodded, looking relieved. Michael pulled out his phone. "Would you like me to call him?"

"Yes, please. Ask him to meet us tomorrow, somewhere he won't feel threatened. I'll trust you to pick a suitable location."

CHAPTER TWO

Adam woke up when the early morning sunshine invaded his cabin. As a teacher, he'd been pretty much forced into being a morning person, and the habit had stuck. Fueling up on oatmeal, he poured a mug of coffee. His wolf didn't like the caffeine, but he should have enough time for it to dissipate before the chore of meeting with the local werewolves. He'd been surprised to hear back from them so quickly, and was slightly concerned they might be trying to pull something on him. The alphas had clearly not been pleased to learn he was in their territory.

They could be setting a trap, but they'd made a point of choosing a location that was remote enough to get to by wolf, yet near enough to town that it was unlikely they'd be willing to make a commotion. Was he giving them too much credit for having thought of that?

He didn't think so. Michael and Linda hadn't been pleased to meet him, but they'd seemed reasonable and intelligent enough, and everything he'd seen of their pack indicated they were too sane to decide to attack him for no reason other than his very presence.

He finished off his coffee, cleaned the dishes and moved to his computer. His life had gradually improved once he'd been able to turn his cell phone into a Wi-Fi hotspot. Computers had once been his life, but years in the woods with limited access had dampened his obsession. He'd never given the online world up completely, taking advantage of libraries and internet cafés when needed, but now he could work from the comfort of his home, and he'd begun to take advantage more and more.

Navigating his way through a new world—that of trying to track down small airplanes in rural Montana—challenged him in a way he hadn't been since he'd first discovered the online world of werewolves, spending hours gleaning all the info he could on them. The security he was running into now was of course much higher and he enjoyed the buzz of the challenge. One path led to another and another until he finally pulled back, rubbed at his neck with one hand while closing the laptop lid with another.

Interesting stuff. He needed to think about how he wanted to share what he'd discovered with the pack, see what they'd make of it. Of course, it was a little awkward since most of what he'd accessed, he'd done so illegally. Ah well, he'd give it some thought while on his way to meet them.

He stood, stretched, and shed his clothes, stepped out onto the front porch. It had taken him a few years to become comfortable with the change, the abandoning of his human skin into that of the wolf. He'd hated and feared the wolf, what he could do in that form, what he thought it might make him do in either form. Eventually he'd come to an uneasy acceptance that he seemed to be mostly himself no matter what form he was in, and while he was more aggressive and territorial than he'd been as a high school teacher, he'd never had the urge to attack someone for no reason, let alone rape and kill them.

His senses burst with new input, as they always did when he changed. Taking it all in, he found nothing out of the ordinary, no cause for concern. Picking up a tightly rolled pair of sweatpants in his mouth—he had no interest in chatting with them in the nude—he headed into the woods.

About twenty minutes later, he came across a smell that caught his attention. It was faint, but the hint of death drew him in. Approaching the area cautiously, he found no sign of humans, werewolves, or any creature that didn't belong. What he *did* find was a dead wolf. Natural, not like him, and she'd been dead only a few minutes, as far as he could tell. Except, he couldn't tell what had killed her. Did wolves have heart attacks? Just lay down and die? She hadn't been old, but maybe she'd been sick. There was a hint of something...something off, sickly, but he had no idea what it was.

Making a slow circle around her, ever widening, he looked for some explanation. The forest felt wrong, but he wasn't sure how much of that was his human nerves and how much was anything actually being different. He shook his furry head. Wrong, just wrong.

He sneezed, dropping his bundle. He rubbed his snout against his foreleg. It was hotter than he'd realized and he considered going toward the stream. But he'd been following the wolf's trail to see if there were any clues as to why she'd died. He needed to get back to that. Putting his nose up, he scented the air and continued following her back trail.

Another sneeze and he shook his head in annoyance. A rabbit broke free of the brush to his right, racing right in front of his path, and he was off. He was almost on it when he remembered that he'd been doing something. And his pants. Where had he left them? He looked around his back trail. He didn't feel well—hot.

That's right, he'd been going to the stream.

He veered off, coming to a halt at the site of a snarling wolf. The small gray was leaping at him before he had a chance to scare it off. It only took a minute to have the natural wolf on its back, belly bared. But it didn't stop. Didn't stop trying to bite Adam, growling and snapping, foam flying free of his muzzle. Sick.

Hating it but having no choice, he bit deep into the throat between his jaws, jerking until the snap sounded and the body beneath him went still.

Backing away from the dead animal, he turned, looking for a new threat. Bad, something bad was in his forest. He heard a sound, far off, and paused. A slight scent on the breeze from the direction of the noise had him off and running. Werewolves. On his land.

Their fault?

Red-hot anger fueled his race toward the danger. These were his woods, his wolves, and he would protect them or die.

He didn't try to mask his approach. Bursting through the underbrush, he came to a stop and watched the intruders. He sneezed, irritated that they smelled wary but not afraid. They should be afraid. A vague sense of memory nagged him, but he pushed it aside as he assessed the threat. A mix of strength and power. He growled, long and low, warning them off. One chance was all he was willing to give.

Myra had dreamed of her husband last night. Not the nightmare she'd had many times over the years, that moment when her soul had shattered and she'd dropped to her knees while making breakfast, certain in the knowledge that her mate was dead. No, she'd dreamed about the first time they'd met. Eric had been on vacation, passing through St. Louis on a long road trip with a couple of his buddies after they'd graduated college. The trio had stopped in to pay their respects to the alpha, her father. Myra had still had a year left in school herself, so he'd moved to her pack, insisting he could be a police officer in any major city but it would be silly for her to transfer colleges when she was so close to being done.

Of course, there hadn't been any question that they would be together. They were werewolves, and they'd known within minutes of meeting each other that they belonged together. Well, maybe she'd had a little nervous doubt, a wondering if it was just wishful thinking that the handsome young man wanted her. But he'd been just as excited, and just as eager to be sure. He'd gotten them a room at a fancy hotel and made long, sweet love to her. They'd bonded, and she thought she'd never be happier in her life. Then he'd fucked her senseless and she'd realized she didn't know from happy yet.

And she'd been right. Every day they were together was just better and better.

She looked out the car window, suppressing a sigh, thankful that Michael was respecting her need for quiet. It was rare for her to think so much about Eric anymore. Which almost felt like a betrayal. For the first hours, she'd been nearly catatonic. For the first days, completely inconsolable. For the first months, she'd been withdrawn, trying to convince her heart that it was important to keep on beating, to keep making it through, day by day. The first years she'd not gone a day, an hour, without thinking about him.

Finally, after four years, she'd seen the sadness she felt every day mirrored in an older wolf, a widower. They'd had sex with the full knowledge that each was thinking of another, each was wishing they were with someone else. She'd cried afterward and the man had held her until they'd both fallen asleep. He'd been gone by the time she'd woken.

There'd been others through the years, each time less painful than the last.

Shaking off the memories, she concentrated on the here and now. Adam deserved her full attention. Focusing, she actually looked out the window she'd been staring through for half an hour, since their conversation had stilled and she'd had the opportunity to remember her dream. She'd been to many forests in the United States, all beautiful. She never tired of their differences, just as she always enjoyed their similarities. Michael pulled the truck into a narrow turnoff and glanced at her. When she smiled, he offered one in return and they got out, walked into the woods, their pace brisk but nearly silent.

It was different, walking in the woods in her human form. And not something she did very often. This was the wolf's territory, her realm. But it was important to appear as nonthreatening as possible to Adam. Not that she couldn't hold her own in this form or change with a speed that only the most powerful werewolves could accomplish. He might know that, but would still understand that she was intentionally being non-aggressive.

An uneasy silence descended and she came to a stop, Michael at her side. She took a deep breath and closed her eyes, listening, scenting. The air was heavy with the scent of pine and the loam blanketing the forest. Something had disturbed the wildlife, and she didn't think it was them. One look at Michael confirmed that he shared her uneasiness. He unbuttoned his flannel shirt and made sure his sneakers were loose.

Michael pointed north. "The meeting point is about half a mile that way."

She nodded, but in silent agreement they headed east, where their senses were pointing them.

It wasn't long before the unmistakable sounds of an approaching predator, who didn't care if he was detected, brought them to a halt. Myra stood still and waited while Michael kicked off his shoes and unbuttoned his pants. He'd just pulled his shirt off when the huge black wolf skidded into view and sneezed. Somehow the action in no way diminished the danger the wolf presented. He watched them warily, waiting for their response.

Myra sent out a wave of power, along with some calm, toward him. He responded with raised hackles and crouched for attack.

She gave Michael a nod, knowing he was waiting for her signal before turning. The power of the change prickled over her skin, but her attention was on the wolf in front of her. He made a tiny movement that signaled attack, so she pushed a stronger wave of power at him, and a single word, "Stop."

His growls increased and she could feel the rage slashing through the air between them, but he didn't move. His body fairly vibrated in his attempt to push through her command. She backed it up with more power, more strength as she held a hand out to her side, signaling for Michael to keep his position. He huffed in agitation but held firm.

Adam—she was sure it was Adam, there couldn't possibly be another alpha werewolf around without their knowledge—was struggling against her hold. "Stand down." Her most dominating voice, along with another swell of power, had an effect, but not as strong as it should have. She reached out with her senses, trying to understand what was happening.

Sick. There was a slight smell, but more it was the psychic feel of him that was off. Just like Michael had described, only this time, instead of an average member of the pack, the infected wolf was a strong alpha. His eyes were wild, his breathing harsh and she didn't think he even recognized Michael. Not good. She needed to end this, and she needed to do so quickly.

Myra reached inside herself, finding the connections she had with the strongest pack alphas she knew. Tapping into the bonds, she pulled, letting their combined powers wash through her. It wasn't something she'd ever tried to do, but she had no choice. The longer she challenged the wolf, the more he resisted submitting to her, the more dangerous the situation.

She pushed out, taking a step forward, Michael at her side giving a low whine as he felt the periphery of the power she sent forth. The black wolf gave one long, continuous growl, but was unable to move against them. His fury beat at her but it was the spark of fear that nearly rattled her. He wasn't afraid of *her*. He wasn't afraid of dying or being hurt. He was afraid of being dominated, compelled to do something that he didn't want to do. And she had no choice but to force his submission.

Her heart ached but her power remained steady. She took another step forward. He tried to retreat, but couldn't even do that. The closer she got, the stronger his growls, until he was shaking with them. She tried to connect with him, tried to find the man within, might have been able to if he were a wolf she had a bond with. Meeting his gaze full on, she pulled on the power again, held it tightly around herself as she lowered to her knees at his side.

His growls turned to whines and he didn't move a muscle. She reached a hand out and grabbed him by the scruff of the neck, pulling sharply to emphasize her domination. His entire body went slack and his eyes closed. His breathing was still harsh but she felt his fear receding in the face of his capitulation. It had been a long time since she'd felt that herself, the utter relief of finally giving in to someone of greater power. He tilted his head slightly, careful not to dislodge her hand but offering his neck.

She used the power she was holding, refocusing it. "Turn, now."

A massive shudder racked his strong body. She stroked down his back as the hair began to recede and the man came forth. He cried out, and she used the connection she was slowly building to ease some of the pain that the sickness must be causing. A forced change would never be comfortable, but it shouldn't be hurting him.

Fully changed, he was on his knees in front of her, his braced arms shaking. He watched her from light brown eyes that were dull with pain and confusion. She moved her hand up his muscled back and gave a gentle tug toward her.

He collapsed into her and passed out.

She pushed the sweaty hair back from his forehead as Michael changed next to her. The other man moved slowly back to his clothes and returned while tugging on his shirt, clearly tired from the back-and-forth shifting.

"He has a fever," she said. "I'm having a hard time connecting with him."

Michael knelt down beside them and reached a hand out to the sleeping man's side. Touch was important to werewolves, and an alpha was compelled to take care of the weaker, the sick, even if they weren't his pack. Adam shifted restlessly under the other man's touch, though, and Michael pulled back.

"That's what my wolves felt like, hot and impossible to connect with." He nodded back the way they'd come. "I have some extra sweatpants in my truck."

"You said the pack doctor wasn't able to do anything other than treat the fever, right? You have any Tylenol in your first-aid kit?"

"Yeah, I'll grab that, too."

"Thanks."

While Michael loped back to the vehicle, Myra considered her options. She needed to decide what would be best for a wolf she'd never spoken to. Stay out here until he woke up, probably still weak and sick, based on what Michael had told her about his wolves; send

Michael out to see if he could track Adam's scent to his cabin, thereby invading his privacy; or take him to a pack location where he might feel captured and surrounded.

In the end, there wasn't really a choice. She wouldn't do anything more than she'd already done to force the man's compliance. She might as well get comfortable.

She focused her senses on him, letting the hand on his forehead slide into his dark brown hair, analyzing what she could sense of him. His sleep wasn't deep. She fed him a slow but steady stream of power, not trying to heal him since she didn't know what was wrong, but giving him strength.

His muscles were hard and defined, though not bulky. He was lean, and probably about her age.

Her sharp ears picked up a sound indicating Michael was on his way back. The man lying across her lap stirred, a nearly soundless growl vibrating through her.

"Shh, it's okay. You're safe."

The only response was a huff of breath, but Adam relaxed again.

Michael jogged into the clearing and set the pants down next to her, hunkering down to be at her level. "We wait?"

She considered. "I think you should head back. Make sure there were no other outbreaks of this...whatever this is."

He shook his head. "I have my cell, I would have heard by now."

"Good point. I have mine, as well. Head back, and I'll call when I need a ride. I'm going to try and talk him into letting me help him back to his place, and he's probably feeling too vulnerable right now to invite two alphas home."

"I can leave you the truck. I'll head back toward the house, call for a ride in a couple of miles, so he doesn't get upset by more arrivals."

"That works, thank you." She lifted up slightly to pull her cell phone from her back pocket, made sure she had reception. Only two bars, but it would do. "I'll update you in an hour, no matter what."

He hesitated. "You're sure?"

She nodded. "I'm sure. I'll call you."

Adam stirred twenty minutes later. Left to his own devices, he probably would have rolled over and gone back to sleep, but Myra had other plans. She moved her hand to his neck, resting it there lightly.

"Adam." She didn't say it loudly, but strongly.

His eyes opened a slit and focused immediately on her. Tension rang through his body but he didn't move. She tightened her hold on him and he relaxed some.

"I need you to get up now, Adam, so we can get you home." He blinked at her and rolled his eyes to the side, realizing they were out in the woods. His gaze glanced down to his naked self, lying on the ground, curled around a strange but dominant wolf's fully clothed body. She was watching for it, so the tiny spark of fear that he carefully shook off was plain to her. Her thumb brushed over his neck and she leaned down close to his face, her eyes steady on his.

"I've got some pants for you. We can either hang out here in the woods a while, or we can walk about fifty yards to Michael's truck, and you can give me directions to drive you home. Your choice."

His breathing was a bit faster than it should be but he moved slowly, cautiously rolling up off her lap, his eyes going to the pants at her side. She scooped them up, held them out to him. He took the offering, stood, stumbled, righted himself quickly, and pulled on the pants. Myra rose slowly.

"Truck." The word seemed to stick in his throat a bit and he coughed, but he was already looking stronger than he had just moments before. Pleased, Myra didn't give him a chance to stagger through the woods on his own. She stepped forward, wrapped an arm around his waist and motioned in the direction they needed to go.

He stiffened, blinked at her, gave his head a tiny shake. Together they walked, his body still warm with fever, his steps uneven, his hold on her firm. He was about three inches taller than her five-foot-five frame and probably had twenty pounds on her, but they managed well enough.

She got him to the passenger door and he sagged against the truck while she opened it. "Are you well enough to direct me to your cabin?"

The affronted look he gave her was pure male and she had to bite her lip to keep from smiling. He hauled himself into the truck and leaned his head back, his face slick with sweat. He pointed up the road and closed his eyes. She worried he'd fall asleep and she'd just keep driving, but then again, that wasn't really a bad thing. But he grunted out the occasional directions and before too long, she was pulling up to a small but well-maintained log cabin. Clothes strung along a line swayed slightly in the breeze. What looked to her untutored eyes like a vegetable garden spanned the length of one wall.

He got out of the truck before she made it around to him, but didn't resist when she tucked herself to his side. She supported most of his weight up the stairs and was relieved to find the door unlocked. Inside, there was a neatly made bed along the back wall and she headed straight for it, ignoring the rest of the surroundings.

Adam fell onto the bed, face first, and didn't move. She shoved him over to the far side, pulled the covers down on her side, then dragged him back over to free the rest. Pulling just the sheet up, she draped it up to his hipbones, then checked his forehead. Burning up.

Turning, she surveyed the one room cabin.

There was a small kitchenette, an open door that showed the bathroom, a closed door that was probably a closet, a fireplace with a small couch and chair situated in front of it, and books. Lots and lots of books.

She glanced back at the bed and saw that he hadn't moved an inch and his eyes were still closed. Filling a glass with water, she shook two tablets from the bottle Michael had given her and set them on a table near the bed. A quick trip to the bathroom procured a washcloth and towel. The water from the tap didn't warm up and it took her a minute to realize it wasn't going to. As much of her life as she'd spent in the woods, it hadn't been at places that didn't have gas, electricity and phone lines.

She squeezed as much of the cold water out of the cloth as she could before bringing it to his body. He jerked at the first contact, but soothed easily as she ran the cloth around his sweaty chest, arms and face. She tried to think like a nurse, rather than a woman who hadn't had sex in nearly a year. Yeah, right. Deciding he didn't need to be wiped down below the waist, she left the sheet where it was, nipping temptation in the bud.

Easing a hand under his head, she picked up the pills.

"Adam, you need to take some Tylenol."

He grunted.

She lifted his head and his eyes opened to slits again, an adorable glare on his face.

She smiled sweetly and shoved the pills against his lips, then followed quickly with the water glass when he opened his mouth. He swallowed, managed another grunt, and turned his head away when she lowered it back to the pillow.

She watched him for a time, wiped him down again with the cloth.

When she moved away, he shifted restlessly but settled down quickly. She walked outside, leaving the door open so she could still see him. Michael answered on the first ring and she assured him that she was fine, Adam was sleeping, and the cabin was more than adequate. She spoke to the pack doctor for a few minutes, but learned nothing new.

Back inside, she surveyed her options. There were no window coverings, so no way to keep the bright afternoon light from bathing her patient. She went into the kitchen and found a couple of cans of chicken noodle soup, setting them aside for later. A quick search produced a can opener, bowls and pan. She made a mental note to be sure to fix the soup before she lost the light coming in through the windows, rather than deal with cooking by the light of a lantern.

She dragged the reading chair to the side of the bed, set another glass of water on the bedside table, and picked out a book. Curling up on the chair, she opened the book but found her gaze on the sleeping man, rather than the pages. His rest seemed healthier now, though she wasn't sure how much of that was reality and how much her fancy. He breathed deep and evenly and he was no longer flushed.

He had the muscles of someone who worked his body hard on a daily basis. What did he do out here all day? Obviously, he'd chopped the logs by the fire, and she guessed there was an even larger stack of them somewhere outside. He worked his garden, certainly. And he read. But what else? She couldn't even begin to imagine. Certainly, she enjoyed her solitude on occasion. It was the thing she looked forward to the most as her busy year as National President came to a close. But she also knew that after her return to normalcy, to life without the additional demands of her term, she'd be eager to surround herself with pack. With family and friends.

Adam stirred, his hand coming up to scratch lightly at his chest before settling back down. His long fingers rested in the light dusting of hair surrounding one nipple and she stared at it a bit hungrily before blinking.

What the hell was wrong with her? The poor man was sick and she was lusting after his body. To be fair, it was a mighty fine body, but still.

That was another reason he shouldn't be holing himself away in the lonely cabin. He needed to find his mate. A stab of jealousy at that idea surprised her, and had Myra tearing her gaze away from the sleeping man and forcing her concentration to the book.

CHAPTER THREE

Adam woke biting back a scream. He refused to give them the pleasure of his screams. He shook his head, grimacing at the dull throbbing he became aware of, and forced his eyes open. It took him a second to understand why the scene looked wrong. He was in his cabin, not in Arizona.

Flashback. Jesus, he hadn't had a flashback in a long time. Still, something nagged at him, insisting there was more wrong than the nightmare reminder of when he'd become a monster.

Scrubbing at his face, he swung his legs over the side of the bed, jerking free of the tangling blankets, amazed at how weak he felt. He smelled rank. Like fear and desperation. More than the flashback could account for. And he felt like shit. A quick glance around the room didn't produce any clues, but a slight scent made its way to his nose around his own stink. A woman's scent.

A quick flash of memory...of wavy brown hair, piercing dark eyes and strong, supportive arms. He'd been sick, and she'd been taking care of him.

He stumbled over to turn on the switch for the hot water, collapsed onto the dining room chair to wait.

His stomach roiled as the memory of meeting her in the woods struck him. She was a wolf. She was dominant. She'd controlled him.

Sheer force of will was the only thing that kept the soup and water she'd been feeding him from re-emerging. Fuck. No wonder he'd had a flashback to Arizona. To when that prick Cage had abducted him, chained him to a wall and turned him into a monster. It was the last time he'd allowed something to happen to him without his control.

Until now.

Until her.

Shit.

He took another look around the small cabin but there was nothing to indicate where the woman might be. Forcing his brain to work despite the headache, he tried to remember what had happened before he'd run into her and the local alpha. He hadn't exactly been in control then, had he? No matter how hard he tried to focus, he could only remember smelling intruders and being certain they were up to no good. He'd been ready to attack, but was pretty sure he'd managed to give them a warning, give them a chance to escape. If they'd run, he'd have let them go. He hoped.

But they hadn't run. They'd faced him down, and they'd won. *She'd* won. Put him on the ground like a newborn pup. Fuck.

Forcing his stiff body to stand, he decided to forget about what had happened and focus on the now. Yeah, right. He didn't believe the lie even as he issued the order. Still, he dragged himself to the shower and stood under the warm spray, wishing it was harder. His whole body went on alert when he heard a sound over the water.

The woman— Myra, she'd told him her name was Myra—was moving around in the cabin, but she didn't come close to the bathroom door.

Rage and fear teased him but he forced them away, forced his muscles to relax. He needed better control before confronting her. Either he'd attack and kill her, or she'd put him down again. Neither option was something he was willing to let happen, so he'd stay in the shower a while and hope he could get hold of himself.

Control. They'd taken it from him, turned him into an animal, but he'd escaped. And he'd vowed he would never allow himself to lose it again, either to another person or to the beast inside. In the early days, after turning, after escaping, he'd had plans for how he'd kill himself if he thought he was losing control. He'd run as far away from civilization as he could manage. Avoided all people for a time before he'd trusted himself to make limited forays into the populated world. Until he'd trusted himself enough to keep control.

For years now, it hadn't been a big concern. Had he become complacent? So sure he'd created a life where he could manage the beast that he'd somehow let it slip, let it slowly take over?

When he heard the front door close, he turned off the water. Straining his ears, he could detect no sound or movement in the cabin. Exhausted, he carelessly swiped a towel over his body, rubbed his hair briskly, then wrapped it around his hips. He wasn't surprised to find the cabin empty. But he *was* surprised to find the bed remade with fresh sheets.

Most likely he should be upset. Furious and territorial. Right now, he could barely manage to remain upright. He felt like he'd been asleep for a month and needed another week. He knew it hadn't been long, only because his stubble wasn't that bad. He glanced out the window and saw it was full dark. All day then. Well, he'd been completely at her mercy for hours, and so far as he could tell, she'd only fed him and cleaned up after him. Still, it didn't change the fact that she'd had complete control over him. And still could.

He made himself go to the kitchen, pull out the cold cuts. Though he didn't quite have the energy to make a sandwich, he forced himself to eat the whole package of meat. A hungry werewolf was not a great idea. He'd been hungry the first time he'd turned. Ravenous. They hadn't fed him for the day and a half he'd been held captive, before the full moon. So he'd already been hungry and hurt. He'd never really be sure how long he'd been a beast before he came back to himself, the remains of a deer at his feet.

Flashes from that night had haunted his dreams for a long time, visions of his attackers stumbling back from his enraged wolf, of the blood that had coated him when he'd finally stopped long enough to take a look. How much of it was from the freaks who'd abducted him and how much was from the deer, he was careful not to consider.

Pulling the sheets back, he dropped the towel and climbed into bed. He should fight. He should run. There were plenty of forests in the United States. No reason he had to stay here. Every reason to leave. He rubbed at his gritty eyes and tried to figure out what the best plan was.

THE SCENT of something sweet and tantalizing drew Adam from sleep again. Before he'd figured out what it was, or recognized that someone else was in the room with him, a hand touched his shoulder and he reacted.

He grabbed the hand and rolled his body, knocking the intruder to the ground and covering her body with his. She made a slight sound of pain or surprise, and he froze. Somewhere in the midst of the fall, he'd realized who it was. Had he hurt her? Had she been about to hurt him? She'd been helping him, he reminded himself.

Underneath him, she was soft and still, not fighting back. He met her clear brown gaze. She wasn't afraid. That was good, wasn't it? He didn't want to scare her, he just didn't want her to hurt him. Control him. He tried to take a deep breath to clear his head—and realized his mistake when her scent filled him. Sweet and clean and hot. Jesus. His dick came to attention and he buried his nose in her hair, gave a tiny lick to her neck.

Taste exploded on his tongue. Unable to resist, he traced the line of her jaw until he reached her chin, gave it a quick nip, then found her lips. He traced them, as well, though she opened for him immediately. She lifted her head, trying to draw him in, but he made her wait. Her hands came up to his shoulders and pulled him closer. Her body under his was warm and compliant, making him want—

He froze. Compliant?

Blinking away the lust he'd let rule his mind, he forced himself to concentrate. Pulling back, he stared at her. Her body tightened, but only for a second, before she relaxed again. She met his gaze and he waited for her to do something. To overpower him, physically or mentally, he was ready for either. But she didn't move, just stared at him softly.

This wasn't right. She wasn't being submissive. Wasn't lowering her gaze or giving him her throat. But neither was she demanding he do the same. Hell, she wasn't even demanding he get off her body. The mental puzzle was enough to pull him back from his instincts. The ones that had started off defensive and leapt into lustful. Damn, he'd only ever worried about rage controlling him, never lust.

He moved off her slowly, not backing down, but giving them both space. Crouched a few feet from her, he waited. She sat up carefully, keeping eye contact.

"Hello, Adam. You're looking much better." She tugged her shirt down from where it had ridden up slightly, and he had to fight not to follow the motion with his eyes.

"Myra."

She nodded. "I wasn't sure how much you'd remember."

He gestured to the couch and she smiled and broke eye contact. His senses on high alert, he gave her his back, going to the dresser for sweatpants while she took a seat. When he turned, she'd made herself comfortable, curling her bare feet up on the cushions beneath her thighs, her weight leaning on the couch arm. Not in any way defensive. Was she so sure he wouldn't attack? Or so sure she'd easily be able to stop him if he did?

He couldn't stop the low growl that rumbled from his throat, which brought a wary look to her face. Maybe she wasn't as carefree as she was making out.

"Would you like me to leave?" she asked. "You could come meet me at Michael's house, or somewhere more neutral. We do need to talk, but I'm not here to cause you any trouble."

He shouldn't need the reminder that something was going on, something he needed to deal with. He wasn't going to hide from the problem, even if it meant working with people and situations that made him uncomfortable. Unless...could the woman and Michael be the ones who were responsible for the sick wolves? There was one simple way of knowing for sure, and that was asking Michael. He was more powerful than the alpha. But now he was afraid. Afraid the woman was more powerful than *he* was, and could force him to...what? Or had she only been stronger than him because he'd been sick?

He focused his attentions on her without meeting her eyes. She would most likely know what he was doing, but she wasn't worried. It only took a minute to decide, yes, she was more powerful than he was. But not hugely so. He wasn't sure what that really meant. Could she force him to do something he really didn't want to do when he wasn't out of his head?

He was being an idiot. Being more powerful than someone else didn't automatically make you evil. He'd never forced his will on another wolf. In fact, other than the incident in Arizona, he'd never seen it done when it hadn't been necessary. Like an alpha helping a younger wolf maintain control. And he had to admit, that was what the woman, Myra, had done. Helped him keep from attacking.

He shook his head and got up to start a pot of coffee. He had been out of control, not because of Michael and the woman, but because of whatever was going on in the woods. He knew that, but still, she made him wary.

She didn't react to his abrupt movement to the kitchen area, didn't pester him for an answer. She seemed content to wait him out and by the time he had two mugs of coffee, he was calmer.

He brought the coffee to her, despite certain instincts telling him not to get that close. She reached for the mug he offered with a dazzling smile. "Thank you so much." His answering grunt wasn't his finest moment, but she didn't seem too bothered by it. He sat in the chair and took a deep breath.

"What happened to me? What's happening in the woods?"

She blew carefully on her drink but didn't take a sip. "I'm not sure. Michael thinks wolves are being poisoned. Two of his people were affected as well. They reacted as you did, but they were younger wolves, not as strong. Michael called the National Council for help. You know what that is?"

"Why don't you start from the beginning, so I don't misunderstand anything." He wasn't going to share that he'd hacked into their website.

She frowned a bit, but continued. "There are something like two hundred packs in the country. They each have a territory that belongs to them, that they're responsible for. Some are small areas with large populations and some are large areas with smaller populations. It just depends on the location. Each pack has an alpha, or an alpha pair," she continued, watching to see how much he understood. When he nodded, she continued. "Then there's the hierarchy. The first, second, third and fourth. Each position can be held singly, or by a mated pair. Mated pairs have the same power level as each other."

Again, she paused and he nodded for her to continue.

"There is a similar structure on a national level. Members of the hierarchy of all packs are elected to serve on the National Council. Only one wolf holds each position, even if they're mated. The post is for one year."

"And what kind of authority does this council have?"

"Absolute, as far as it goes. Only the more powerful alphas are elected. The position has the effect of bumping up your power level. Which means that for one year, the National President is more powerful than any other wolf."

"That sounds dangerous to me."

She pursed her lips. "I can see how it would. And of course, there is the potential for something to go wrong. But it's actually pretty low. Along with the power boost comes the connection with your wolves."

He frowned and she sighed. "You don't know what that means. I was afraid of that."

He didn't say anything, not sure what the best play was and figuring silence would serve him for now.

"I've been down in Arizona," she started, but it was already too much for him. It was the last thing he'd expected her to say.

He stood, stalked past her and through the front door. He kept part of his attention on the cabin, on the wolf who hadn't threatened him overtly but had brought his fear alive again with five simple words. But he scanned the woods in the early morning light, his land, using his eyes, ears and nose to prove to himself that nothing was wrong in the immediate area. Nothing but him.

After a couple of minutes, he ran his fingers through his hair, took a deep breath, and faced the cabin. She stood in the doorway, watching him with sympathy.

He narrowed his eyes. What did she know to be feeling sympathetic? Well, she'd said she'd been to Arizona, so maybe she knew everything. Which meant…what?

"Arizona," he prompted.

She moved out onto the porch and lowered herself to the step, wrapping her arms around her knees. He wondered if the move was meant to make her appear less dangerous. Not that she appeared dangerous at all. That was only an instinct, and it wasn't fooled at all by her new position.

"Yes. A wolf out in Idaho found his mate recently, and discovered that she'd been attacked by a werewolf and forcibly turned."

He couldn't keep the tension from his body, knew she'd be as aware of it as he was. "Is that right? That kind of thing happen a lot?"

Her face softened even further, and now there was sadness in those eyes. "No. No, it doesn't happen very often at all. Which is why I was called in to deal with it."

"Because you're on this council?"

"This year's National President."

Well. "They called in the big guns, huh?"

"Some very tough decisions had to be made, and nobody else could make them."

"Why don't you just cut to the chase and tell me what you came here to tell me."

"All right. Hillary told us she'd been taken to a ranch out in Arizona, where she was attacked and raped and held until the full moon. She managed to keep from turning until the pack thought she wasn't going to make it and left her to die. Then she turned and made her escape."

His knees felt a bit wobbly, but he locked them tight, leaned back against a tree.

"Hillary stayed away from other werewolves for the next four years, so we knew nothing about it. As soon as I found out, I went to the pack that covers the territory she was taken to. I discovered that the pack had gone bad, knew they had a rogue contingent, but hid their heads in the sand. They were willing to let these atrocities stand rather than call for help."

Adam kept his eyes focused on Myra's fingers, which had turned white from clenching her legs so tightly. There was a barely banked fury in her voice that he wondered at.

"Atrocities?" he managed to ask.

"It's the tamest word I can come up with right now." She cleared her throat but it was still husky with anger when she continued. "What these wolves did was not only evil, it was downright stupid. It's not how humans are turned into werewolves. The chances of success are minimal, and if they do manage to find someone strong enough to survive the turn, there's zero chance that person will just meekly accept a place in that pack, under an insane alpha."

"Is that right?"

She dropped her hands and stood, facing him more fully. "Adam, I'm not here to be coy. I interrogated both packs, the legitimate and the rogue. I disbanded both packs. I decided who would live and who would die. And when I found out that another victim had survived, had made the change and escaped, I knew I wouldn't rest until I found him."

"So you can decide if *he* should live or die?"

Her shock was real and unmistakable. "No!" She scrubbed her

hands over her face, said more quietly, "No. So that I could tell him that while I could never make right what had happened to him—to *you*—that the bastards have been taken care of and won't be hurting anyone ever again."

"That's good to know. Thanks for stopping by." He didn't bother to move, knew it wasn't that simple. Not after what had happened. Not after he'd almost attacked her and Michael. Without real provocation.

"We'd begun looking for you but weren't having much luck. Michael had called in a report about the trouble you all are having out here, and we would have sent someone down to help check it out. But when you came forward he remembered I had sent out a request for information on a strong, unknown wolf, so here I am. I'm thankful we've found you, but I'm sorry it's taken something bad happening for us to meet." She gestured to the woods behind him. "But we can help each other. I'm getting the sense you care about your land. The animals on that land. Even if you don't get poisoned again, does it bother you that the natural wolves are dying? And that they're dying badly?"

A growl slipped free of his throat. She smiled, though it was of the joyless variety. "That's kind of what I meant before, about the connection the National President has with their wolves. It's similar, though much deeper, than what you probably feel for the local natural pack. I'm sure you've seen it in action, if you think about it. You've probably felt it. You're a strong wolf, your natural instinct is to take care of those weaker than you are, which is most wolves that you meet."

He did know what she meant, now that she'd pointed it out. Had felt it most strongly with the wolves that roamed near his cabin, but remembered following a pair of drunk teenage girls, shifters, around town until they'd been collected by a stronger wolf, someone he now realized was probably in their pack's hierarchy. He'd called himself a fool, told himself he was being a creepy stalker, but he just couldn't walk away until he'd been sure the girls were safely in the hands of someone who could see to their welfare.

There had been other instances, a wolf he'd come across in Kansas, a young man who'd managed to break his leg while alone in the woods. He'd been irritated, but unable to walk away without seeing the wolf to safety. Because he was the stronger wolf, the one in control. Which, reminded him he owed her an apology.

"I'M SORRY," told her, gruffly. "About earlier."

Myra felt herself blush. "No, I should apologize."

Adam blinked, stared at her for a moment. "I lost control."

"I think you showed amazing control. Waking up, after being so sick, to someone touching you, but you controlled the situation, didn't hurt me, while making sure you could protect yourself." She sat back on the porch step again.

"I meant...the other part." He rubbed the back of his neck wearily. "Are you so powerful that you weren't even nervous I would overpower you?"

"When a strong, naked, attractive wolf is lying on top of me—" She cleared her throat. "Again, I'd say I'm the one who should apologize. I shouldn't have encouraged you. I've been here, helping you, watching you, and...well, you've been sick, mostly asleep...so it's inappropriate...I...you—"

"Jesus, stop," he interrupted her.

She cleared her throat. "Anyway, no need for you to apologize to me." She stood. "You should eat. I still have Michael's truck. We could go into town, get some breakfast. Or to the pack house. Unless you'd rather..." She gestured to the woods.

He looked over his shoulder, turned back to her with a questioning look. "How bad would it be if *you* got infected with this poison?"

She froze, didn't even breath while the implications of that raced through her brain. Her panic at the thought must have been strong enough to transmit through the bonds she held, because she received some faint, questioning impressions. Forcing in a deep breath, she blew it out and sent back as much a feeling of calm as she could. She'd need to spend some time on the telephone soon. For now, she just nodded.

"Yeah, that would be pretty bad."

"Then we'll stick to town. As far as I know, everyone who's gotten sick has been in the woods."

They went into the cabin. He moved to the dresser and pulled on jeans and a sweater while she gathered the little bag that held her essentials. Michael had brought it last night, meeting her nearby. She pulled out the car keys and they headed out. As they approached the truck, she sensed Adam's hesitation.

"Would you prefer to drive?"

"You wouldn't mind?"

"Not at all." She held out the keys, met his eyes as he took them from her. Whatever she could do to give him security and safety, she was happy to do.

They were on their way, and she held her silence to match his.

"What's it like, how's it different, living with the pack?" he asked, after a time.

"Well, you have to understand, I was born and raised as a werewolf, I've never known different. But, current statistics are that we're about seventy-five percent born wolves, and twenty-five percent turned. And whenever a turned wolf joins a pack, we all make an effort to help them through any confusion, so I think I have a fair idea of what is different."

"Turned. Maybe you could tell me about that." His hands flexed on the steering wheel.

"Okay." She twisted a bit so that she was looking at him. "What happens is that a wolf meets someone that they believe to be their mate. Their alpha will confirm the connection and help the wolf explain about being a shifter."

He grunted. "That must be interesting."

She smiled. "I've only done it a couple of times. The thing is, it's not about logic. There's magic involved."

The look he turned to her managed to convey skepticism perfectly.

"No, really. Seriously, how else can you explain that your body shifts into a wolf? I mean, your very bones reshape themselves, how is that not extraordinary and magical?"

He gave a grudging nod.

"My point is, it's not like regular humans. Mates coming together, it's an amazing thing, something most humans are never able to experience, and that is terribly sad to me."

He glanced at her but didn't say anything. She cleared her throat and went on. "So while, in the abstract, it sounds ridiculous explaining that to someone you've just met, in reality, they're feeling the pull, the connection, the magic, just as the wolf is. Plus, once someone changes to show them, so they can't argue the reality of it, things tend to simplify."

"And if someone chooses not to change?"

She nodded. "It's rare, but of course not impossible. Sometimes the wolf doesn't get over it. Some can have sex, relationships even, but never find another mate. Others are lucky enough to find another mate, though it's usually many years later. Again, the whole scenario is pretty rare, so there aren't a lot of examples to learn from."

He braked the truck as they came to another road and he started to turn toward the town. "I thought wolves mated for life. How can they find another one?"

"We do mate for life. And we live slightly longer than humans. But if you haven't actually mated, that's different. But once you *have* mated, there's no straying, no desire to seek out someone else, no need to worry about losing that connection."

"And if one of them dies? Do they just find another mate?"

Her stomach turned, but she forced her voice to stay steady. "That is also very rare. Mostly because we're harder to kill, so if one dies, they've been a mated pair for a very long time. The idea of giving up that piece, that last connection, with your missing mate, I don't think most widowed wolves are capable of that. But there certainly are cases of it happening, when many years have passed." She paused, and maybe the silence was heavy, because he glanced at her but didn't say anything. "I was mated."

His head whipped around to look at her, his foot coming off the gas for just a second before he returned his attention to the road.

"We were young. I was still in college. His name was Eric. We were together for three years when he was killed. He was a police officer and someone shot him right in the head, point blank." She turned back to face the windshield, needing a minute. Then had to swallow back the tears when he quietly laid a hand on her thigh.

This lone wolf who wasn't used to pack, to touch, to comfort of any sort, was offering that to her. She blinked hard. "I like the idea that someone who's lost that love could find it again, but I can't—" She shook her head. "I can't actually imagine it."

She stayed silent as he drove through the little town to a diner. They got out and took seats in the small, warm room that looked more like a house than a restaurant. Once they'd ordered, steak and eggs for both of them, she leaned back against her chair and looked at him. He appeared much better, much healthier. Much more handsome, if it could be believed.

"You look better. How do you feel?"

"Pretty much normal. But very hungry." He glanced around the room surreptitiously. "You guys were thinking poison."

She nodded. "I don't have any other ideas. But, the pack says they haven't run into any humans who could be putting it out."

"Ask them if they've been hearing planes. Small, low-level planes, flying over more frequently than before."

Well, that was interesting. She nodded, frowned. "I'll do that. And need to think about who I can contact to look into that if it *is* the source. How to track—" She broke off as the waiter brought their food. A small family sat at the table behind Adam, who was holding his knife and fork, waiting for her to begin. Smiling, she dug in.

When he'd eaten half the steak, she decided to see if she could get him talking a bit more. Taking a long drink of her soda, she studied him over the rim. It had been embarrassing admitting her attraction to him, and a little bit disconcerting feeling it so strongly while she was having such vivid memories of her time with Eric—meeting him, losing him—but she could hardly help herself. He wasn't just attractive. His strength and integrity shown through to her so much that she was amazed Michael and Linda had questioned it at all.

"Will you tell me a bit about you? Your life?"

He watched her thoughtfully while he chewed. "Tell me again what your plans were, for when you found me."

She blinked. Ouch. Okay, he deserved to be skeptical. "My plans were to make sure you were okay, living a good life. I had hoped that you would have moved on and found a place for yourself in our society, but I was worried, because if that was the case, we'd have heard about you, known about you. So, that was my plan. Find out why you were still anonymous, if you were still alive, and do what I could to make sure you knew you had people who care, who want you to be safe and whole and welcome."

He didn't look convinced. "You said you had to make hard decisions, in Arizona," he reminded her.

"Yes, that's true." She glanced at the family eating and talking behind him, lowered her voice a tad. "Do you want me to tell you that if we'd found you and discovered that you were a madman, who'd somehow managed to stay under the radar but was hurting or killing humans or wolves, that I would have ended you? That is true, I would have. It would have sucked. But I wasn't really concerned about that, it would have been nearly impossible for you to be those things and have remained undetected for so long."

"You mean like Cage and his band of assholes did?"

"Touché." She grimaced, put her knife and fork down. "You're right, but I can only tell you again how rare it is that managed to happen, and while I would have dealt with it had it happened again, with you, I didn't really worry that it might."

"You're so sure you could have handled it?"

She considered sugarcoating it, decided he could handle the

truth. Would need to understand the truth, if he was to accept the life she wanted him to live, one where he was in contact with wolves, if not an active part of a pack.

"Yes, I'm sure. Between my strength and Michael's, what he could pull on from his pack if he'd needed to, and what I can, and did, pull on from the other alphas while I'm National President, it wouldn't have been a fight. Fights between wolves are fairly rare, and they're between wolves of equal strength."

She let him think about that for a minute while she ate a couple of bites.

"That strength, that I have, that I have access to. That you have. With it comes responsibility. It's why the strong amongst us are so driven to help the weaker. It's a compulsion."

He didn't look confused, so she pushed. "You've felt it."

No response.

"Is that why you've stayed away from the packs?"

He stared at her, his face expressionless, but she gave him only patience in return.

He wiped his mouth with a napkin. "Maybe some of it. I wasn't going to risk falling under someone's authority, but yeah. I had no interest in being that authority and I could feel the tug of it, if I was around the younger wolves long enough."

She nodded, took the last bite of her steak.

"That doesn't make you mad?" he asked.

Surprised, she looked back up at him. "I think you earned the right to ease into all of this—if," she added quickly, "you want in at all. My hope is that you do, and that you'll find the peace and comfort that I know you can in a pack, but as long as you aren't harming anyone, I'm not judging your choices."

He paid the bill despite her protests, so she decided it was a good time to try to bring the conversation back to him.

"How do you make a living?"

He held the diner's door open for her, then followed her to the truck, waiting until he'd eased back onto Main Street to glance at her.

"Computers."

"Oh, right, you were a computer science teacher. That's good, then. You were able to do that remotely?"

"Yes."

"You avoided people for a time, but then began to feel more comfortable? Safe?"

He sighed, settled into his seat, one hand on the steering wheel, the other resting on his thigh. She licked her lips.

"For the first year or so, I stayed away. Lived in the woods a lot, stole a bit of camping gear now and then. I don't feel great about that, but it was better than risking hurting someone."

"I understand."

"Eventually I decided I was safe enough to go to the library, access my bank accounts, that sort of thing. I moved around, tried out different areas, ended up here a few years ago."

"What about people? You can't be all alone all the time."

"I wasn't really good company for a long time. Now, I have some people, reconnected with a couple of people from my old life, mostly online, I have…relationships, when I want to."

Since he gave her the side eye, she understood he meant sex, merely smiled.

"You don't need to worry about me," he said, putting both hands back on the wheel. "I'm comfortable with my life. I appreciate that you wanted to check on that, but once this poison business is taken care of, you can cross me off your list of things to handle."

She leaned against her door, pulled one leg up onto the seat and hooked her arm around her knee. "That's great to know. I'm glad." She meant it. Of course, she left a lot of what she meant unspoken, but he wasn't an idiot. He knew full well she wasn't going to be satisfied with that.

"Mmm, hmm."

Laughing, she reached out and pushed his shoulder. "I'm serious! I'm glad you're safe and sane and reasonably content. I'm pleased that I can cross you off my list as an obligation that needed to be fulfilled before I felt right about handing over the presidency." And if that meant any further dealings with him were her business, not National's business, yay for her.

She let that thought run through her body, warming her up from the inside. He wasn't oblivious, was at least partially in tune with her, whether he realized it or not.

He pulled in a breath and turned to look at her, bringing the truck to a stop on the side of the highway. As he watched her, heat came into his eyes. It satisfied her, thrilled her, enticed her.

But he wasn't ready yet. She looked out the window beyond him. "Where are we going?"

He watched her for a minute. "That's the question. Where do you want to go?"

"I've been in contact with Linda and Michael, they'll call me if anything new happens."

CHAPTER FOUR

Adam had begun to ache. Now that he was full of food, rested, feeling restored, he wanted to touch Myra. Feel her underneath him as he had that morning. Explore. She'd convinced him that she hadn't been upset by his loss of control that morning. Didn't mean *he* wasn't upset by it, but if he got her underneath him again, he could, and would, maintain control. And do some of that exploring.

He had to admit, there were some advantages to this shifter thing, because he knew she wanted him, too. Was open to playing. And maybe it made him an asshole, but once he'd heard she'd had a mate, wasn't likely to find another, some of his reservations had fallen away. Did it suck more to have had that, and lost it, than to never have had it at all? Jesus, now he was a damn philosopher.

He grunted and pulled the truck back onto the road, heading toward his cabin, not the alphas' house.

Trust was a slow thing for him, but he had to admit, she'd done everything right so far. Even knowing that she'd handled shit in Arizona, made the tough decisions that had to be made, lessened his concerns about her. About the National Council. Enough that he wanted to let the building heat free, let it burn them up between the sheets. He had a strong suspicion that the two of them together were going to set the cabin on fire, and now that he was actually entertaining the idea, he wanted to get started.

He glanced over, wanting to see her reaction over heading away from the alphas'. She knew. And she wanted. She took off her seat belt and he narrowed his eyes at her, but she scooted herself to the middle seat and buckled back in. Put her hand on his arm.

"Are you okay?"

"Yeah." She didn't seem put off by his near grunt. Left her hand where it was. "I'm sorry about your husband. Mate."

Her fingers curled in a bit harder and he felt a distant wave of sadness, knew it to be hers.

"I'll never be sorry that we had each other. And I always rejoice when a wolf finds their mate, knowing how special that connection is." She leaned back against the seat more fully, so that most of her side was pressed up against him. "I wonder what he would have been like as a thirty-year-old man, forty. What we would have fought about and if we'd have taken up gardening or genealogy or what."

He took one hand off the wheel, gave her knee a comforting squeeze. It was damned weird to be talking about a woman's dead husband while he was driving her to his house to ravish her. But he wanted to hear about it, wanted to comfort her, take care of her even though he knew nothing would make her loss disappear. He soothed his hand lightly around her knee, his arm resting along her warm thigh.

"I want that for you," she said, her voice low. "I want you to find that happiness, that connection."

"I don't know if I'd survive the loss of that," he admitted.

She swallowed loudly enough that he heard it. "It's hard. If we'd been together years longer, I might not have. But we're hard to kill, this was serious bad luck, so chances are pretty good you'd get to old age together. Mated wolves usually pass within weeks of each other, if not hours, when they die of old age."

"Hm."

She smiled, and he caught it in the rearview mirror. They bumped off the road and onto a dirt lane. He slowed, but maybe not as much as he should have, so she snuggled in and rubbed up against him. He was acting like a sixteen-year-old taking his date to the make-out point. But he knew once he got her to a bed, they'd be doing a hell of a lot more than making out. They should have stopped at the store and gotten more food.

Her fingers resting on his arm began to move, rubbing up and down, just a bit. His foot on the peddle got heavier. Her legs spread open a bit wider in invitation. Forcing himself to keep his eyes on the road, he let his hand curl to the inside of her knee, then ease back a bit, up her thigh until his hand was nestled between them. So close to the heat at the center of her jeans, but not quite there. He drew a circle with his thumb and her breathing deepened.

The driveway to his cabin was coming up and he had to slow down in order to take the turn safely with just his left hand, but he did it, refusing to relinquish the hold he had with his right.

She leaned in, put her mouth up against his ear. "I want to know what you taste like," she whispered.

The soft wetness of her tongue drew his earlobe into her mouth and he had to clench his jaw to maintain control, his gaze glued to the cabin and the spot where he needed to stop the truck. As soon as he hit that spot, he threw the truck into park and turned to her. His hands cupped her face, brought her lips to his and his tongue invaded her mouth before the truck had finished rocking.

Her sweet moan of acceptance, of need that matched his own, somehow managed to both soothe him and fire him up. He slid the fingers of one hand up into her hair, tightened his grip though she wasn't trying to move. Her arms came around his shoulders, tried to pull him closer. The damn seat belt cut between them and gave him enough annoyance to remember that they didn't have to be uncomfortable in the truck when there was a cabin with a bed five feet away.

Keeping the hold in her hair, he drew back on the kiss, giving her soft nips on her lips when she tried to pull him back in. He kissed her cheekbone, the corner of her eye. Moved back far enough to meet her gaze.

"Inside."

She nodded as much as she could. "Inside."

He moved back and they both released their belts. He hopped out of the truck, turned to help as she scrambled behind him, took the hand she offered and moved to the cabin. As always, his senses were on alert for anything wrong in his territory, but nothing concerned him. He saw her glancing around as well, her nose twitching in a way that he was slightly appalled to find adorable. He increased his pace, took the steps in one quick leap, and pulled her through the door.

The door slammed shut and he brought his mouth back to hers. She met him fully, her hands scrabbling at his shirt hem until he felt them on his bare skin. He cupped her bottom, used his hands to keep her steady while his body pushed her back, step by step, until the backs of her legs hit the bed. Her hands were curled up under his shirt, around his shoulders, pulling him down on top of her. He caught himself so that he didn't crush her, pulled his mouth free.

"If you let me go, we can get naked."

"Okay, good, naked is good." She released him and went for his belt buckle. He had to laugh, a sound he wasn't much used to. He leaned back, kneeling above her, and took her in. Hair going all sorts of directions; his fault, he was pleased to know. He supposed the color would be called something fancy, like chestnut or copper. He just liked the way it felt in his fingers as he'd feasted on her. Her eyes bright with heat, with need, for *him*.

"Been a while, sweetheart?" he teased, pulling his shirt up over his head. She had the belt off and moved to the button of his jeans.

"Maybe a bit," she laughed, meeting his eyes. "But mostly the credit goes to you for being hot and sexy."

He gave a quick laugh of surprise while she tugged his jeans down his hips. She was unlike any woman he'd ever been with. Ignoring her sound of protest, he slid off the bed, toed off the shoes he'd forgotten about, finished the job with the jeans, taking his boxers with them. Her hand arrowed straight for his cock and he found himself laughing again. Jesus.

"Uh uh." He knocked her hand away. "Your turn."

She did a sit-up and started on the laces of one boot, while he worked the other. They raced, but her fingers were nimbler than his and she was tossing the boot aside seconds before he managed to do the same. She'd pulled her top halfway over her head by the time he was unbuttoning her jeans. Thankful she wasn't wearing a belt, he curled his fingers over the top and dragged them down her hips, with her help. She kicked them off and he swung a leg over, resuming his kneeling position above her.

"You should come down here," she encouraged, her hands gliding up the sides of his legs, curving around to his ass.

He slid down beside her, putting his mouth at the perfect level to suck on a pouty nipple. She arched up, giving him more of her. At the first taste, he was lost. He flicked and sucked, nibbled and tasted, then switched to her other breast, nuzzling the space between gently with his unshaved chin. She fisted her hands in his hair and moaned his name, a sound so sweet he needed to hear it again. He reached a hand down her body, teased her curls, kept going to find her slick and needy.

She moaned his name again and he couldn't help but smile into her breast. He kissed his way up to her mouth while teasing her slick hole with his finger. Her nails scored down his back, the tiny sting urging him on. When his lips found hers, her tongue thrusting into him impatiently, he entered her with his finger. Her hips bucked up into him, wanting more. He complied with another finger and pressed the palm of his hand against her clit.

Tearing her mouth free, she stared up at him, panting, eyes fierce. "I want to suck you."

"Wait your turn." He kissed her again, his fingers fucking in and out of her. She reached down, curled her hand around his, pressed on his fingers until they found the right spot and she shattered, crying out a thin wail. Music to his ears.

He slid down her body, pulled her wet fingers into his mouth, licked them clean, then turned to the source. He licked her opening, pushing in with his tongue against the squeezing of her muscles. Looking up her body, he watched her head thrash back and forth as the orgasm redoubled. He licked up her slit, pulled her clit between his lips and gave it careful attention with his tongue. She sobbed out, her body going lax except for her hand, which had made its way to his hair again and was tugging at him.

Reaching for the table, he fumbled with the drawer.

"Werewolves don't need condoms," she gasped.

He'd read that on the website, but using one was habitual and he'd forgotten. No sexually transmitted diseases, and he would know if she was *in heat*. Applying that term to a human had seemed appalling to him at the time, but now he was thrilled with the benefits. Smiling, he went back to his activities.

He took his time. Nipping at her thigh, lingering kisses along her belly, and up the valley of her chest. He spent long minutes on each breast, feeling her body slowly regain its energy, its need as he enjoyed his journey. He stretched out on top of her, nuzzled into her neck, kissing her throat until he worked his way back to her lips. She opened for him, welcomed him back, accepted his body in the cradle of her legs as she teased her tongue with his. He slid into her, his cock jumping at the first feel of her slickness, her tightness.

He moved, enthralled by the feel of her, the taste of her, the sense of her. He broke the kiss, shook his head, picked up speed, felt the quickening in his balls that signaled impending release. Myra was watching him, and he growled at her, determined to take her over again. He palmed her breast, tweaked her nipple. Her breath caught, and her eyes rolled back. He leaned down to her ear.

"So fucking beautiful."

MYRA FELT the words as much as heard them, growled into her ear almost like an accusation. She couldn't believe that he'd brought her so high, so fast, after her first orgasm. She needed to come again, needed to feel him fall with her. She dug her heels into his ass, lifted up to meet him thrust for thrust, clenched her inner muscles tight.

"Fuck," she heard him whisper, and smiled.

He bit her earlobe and it was there, crashing through her so hard she had to fight to hold on until she heard him shouting in release as well. Then she let go, and flew. She may have blacked out. Or maybe it just felt that way with a ton of male werewolf laying on top of her as she struggled to breathe. Not that she was complaining.

She played with the shaggy ends of his hair—did he hack it off himself with a knife or something?— and tried not to think too hard. For a minute there it had seemed like her soul had shuddered. But then she'd felt Adam pull back just a bit. She didn't blame him for holding himself back when it had become so intense, but was surprised that they'd connected well enough that she'd felt it. Or even that he'd felt the need to do it at all, had felt so much that it had scared him.

He rolled to the side, but he brought her with him, so that she was half laying on top of him. Now it was him playing with the ends of her hair while she scratched idly at his chest.

"That was nice," she teased.

He grunted. "Flowers are nice. That wasn't nice."

"Hmm. It was...excellent."

"Wine is excellent. That wasn't excellent."

"Okay. What was it."

"Phenomenal. Stupendous. Outrageously fucking hot."

She laughed. "Yes, all of those things. Are you sure you weren't an English teacher?"

His eyes went sad as he traced a pattern of circles on her arm but didn't say anything for a minute.

"My brother was going to be an English teacher. He died before he got that far."

"I'm sorry. That must have been very hard for you and your family."

"He was the only family I had left. Turned out to be better that way."

"I guess that's one way of looking at it. I think maybe that's part of why they chose you. Hillary, the other wolf who survived, she didn't have any family left either."

His chest froze beneath her for a moment before he resumed breathing. "It's my fault she got hurt. Raped. Turned."

She looked up at him, didn't like the bleak guilt she saw on his face. She propped herself up on his chest so that he couldn't look away from her, thought about how she wanted to say what needed to be said. His eyes grew wary as he waited.

"I guess so. I'm still working out what Hillary's punishment should be."

His eyes went hard. "Punishment."

"Yes, for not reporting what had happened."

He growled. "Care to explain that?"

"Well, when we went to Arizona, we found a little girl who'd been kidnapped. We think they were holding her until she was old enough to try and turn. Hillary told me it was her fault that Alexis had been taken and her parents killed. If she'd reported the Cages to the police in the four years she'd been free, Alexis wouldn't have been hurt."

"You would blame her for that?" There was real anger in his voice, and his hand on her arm had turned from a caress to a controlled grip.

"No. Would you?"

"Fuck no!"

"Then why would you blame yourself for the same thing?"

He blinked at her. His body, which had tightened, relaxed under her.

"It's not the same."

"Why not?"

"Because I was first."

"How does that change anything?"

"Because if I had stopped them, neither of the girls would have been taken."

"I refer you to your anger a minute ago. You can't have it both ways." She studied him. Cocked her head. "I know what this is. You're sexist."

He stared at her some more, frowning.

Laughing, she nodded. "That's totally what this is. You think because you're a guy, you should have handled it differently than she did." She cupped his cheek with the hand that wasn't propping her up on his chest. "Adam, you did the best you could under extraordinary circumstances. No one blames you for how you handled it. I have the duty of doling out blame, responsibility and punishment here. That is officially my job. I'm telling you there is no blame on you."

He didn't say anything so she knelt up, straddled him. "You should go visit them. They're in Northern Idaho. See for yourself that they're both doing well now, and neither of them holds you responsible, any more than Alexis blames Hillary."

His hands came to her hips. "Maybe."

"I didn't finish telling you about being National President." She stroked her hands up his chest, flexed her fingers into his pecs.

"The most powerful werewolf in the country." He brought his hands up to her breasts, squeezed.

"That's right. Two more weeks." She wrapped her hands over his, squeezed harder. "And then it will be a guy from California."

"Well aren't I the lucky one?" His fingers tugged at her nipples.

"That's what I'm trying to tell you," she agreed, dropping her hands, bracing them on his thighs behind her. She gasped when he tweaked and pulled, felt herself getting wet. But this time she wanted to explore. Taking his hands in hers, she lifted them above his head, their fingers laced, leaned down to nibble along his jaw, up to his ear. She nuzzled into his neck, drew his scent deep into her lungs. His fingers clenched against hers, his muscles tightening in preparation to move.

"No, stay," she whispered. "Let me taste." She licked his neck. "Explore." She worked her way around his chin to the other ear, pulled the lobe between her teeth and bit down gently. "So much to explore."

His hips pressed up, but settled back.

She moved to the hollow of his throat, licked and kissed, then released his hands to bring hers to his shoulders. She explored the shape, the muscles, stroked his skin while tasting the salty sweetness of his collarbone. His hands rested on her sides but nothing more, letting her have her play.

"So much strength." She bit his pec, just above the nipple, hard enough for him to grunt, hard enough to see faint impressions of her teeth when she checked. "So much power." She kissed the spot. "So much integrity." She pulled his nipple between her lips, enjoying the way his fingers pressed into her hips when she released him with a wet pop.

"I'm currently the most powerful werewolf in the country," she reminded him. "And you make me feel weak with need." She braced her hands on his chest, slid her body down, lifting over his hardening shaft, until she could lower her face to his stomach. His hands moved to her wrists, held them gently. She smiled against his stomach, because it didn't feel like restraint. It felt like he needed the point of contact. "Desperate and hungry." She gave only teasing nips this time, kissed his navel.

She pulled gently against his hold, moved her hands down his sides to his hips when he released her. "So very hungry." She spoke with her mouth just above his pubic hair, intentionally heating him with her breath. His powerful thighs pulsed beneath her, his hands going to his sides to grip the sheets.

"Can I taste?" she asked, moving lower, huffing her breath onto his cock. More color had come into it, its length stretching toward her in need.

"Fuck yes."

She looked up at him, saw her heat mirrored in his eyes. Licked her lips.

"Or I could haul you up here and fuck you senseless," he growled.

She smiled hugely. "Let's stick with plan A for now."

"Only if you—" He broke off when she kissed the underside of his dick, followed quickly by a long lick.

She cupped his balls with one hand, explored his length with the other, while teasing the tip with her tongue.

"Fuck."

He tasted magnificent and she wanted more. No more teasing, she took in as much as she could, concentrated on relaxing her jaw, took in a bit more. He growled his approval. She hummed as she explored and tasted, sucked and swirled. She could feel his tension, his thighs bunched under her hands, the near constant growl coming from his throat. When his fingers threaded through her hair, she curled her fingers into his thighs, letting her nails bite in.

"Fuck," he repeated. And then he moved.

He sat up, pulled her in for a hard kiss. She squeezed his cock but he was moving again. Before she could think to react, she was on her knees, hands braced against the wall at the head of the bed.

"Hurry," she panted, looking over her shoulder.

The look in his eyes grew even hotter. Then his hands were back on her, holding her hips tightly as he pushed into her. She tilted, pushed back against his grip, wanting more.

He gave more. Filled her up, blanketed her body with his, his breath hot against her cheek as he moved within her. The pressure built as his body, slick with sweat, moved over her, his hard length hitting all the right places, his muttered curses in her ear sending shivers through her body. Through her soul.

Bracing one hand on the wall next to hers, he reached his other around and found her clit. A gentle caress, then firmer as she gasped, lost control.

"Adam!"

He flattened her to the wall, pressed into her, over her, around her, until all she could feel was him as he groaned her name. They held still for a minute as the aftershocks of her release pulsed around his softening cock and they fought to catch their breaths. He kissed her cheek, the corner of her mouth, then gently pulled back, his hands helping to hold her steady as she turned and slid back down to the bed.

CHAPTER FIVE

Adam lay next to a sleeping Myra and told himself he was not panicking. Not at all. Just because sex with her had been the most amazing experience of his life, just because his heart had felt like it was beating in time with hers and he'd ached to feel her pressed against him, for every part of his body to connect with hers, was no reason to panic. Instead, he needed to focus on what had to happen next. People were in danger and that was the thing to concentrate on right now.

He checked on Myra. She was sleeping peacefully, a satisfied little smile on her face that had his heart doing funny things in his chest. Shaking his head, he looked away. She was exhausted. Probably hadn't slept much while he'd been sick. Sleep was the last thing on his mind.

He turned his attention to the poisonings, considered what he'd learned on the computer before he'd gotten sick. Like puzzle pieces, the bits of information formed and reformed in his brain until he knew which missing pieces he needed to fill in.

Easing out of bed, he pulled the covers up over Myra and grabbed his sweatpants. He pulled his laptop out of the drawer by the sofa and sat down. Explored. Dug. Hacked. Considered. Once he was on the right trail, it really wasn't that hard. Well, as long as one had the skills to go places they weren't supposed to go, delving into bank accounts and email servers that were meant to be safe.

He dug a couple of USB memory sticks out of the drawer, copied several files.

Then he went to the werewolf website, looked for information about the attack and Hillary. He hadn't seen anything the other day, but Myra had made it seem like it wasn't being kept secret and word had to be getting out now that Hillary had joined Mountain Pack.

He found a couple of threads, very new, with people expressing shock, even doubt that it was real, wolves from Idaho just beginning to chime in to verify the story. It seemed the pack was trying to quell some of the more outrageous rumors and get the truth out there. Or at least, the truth as Myra related it, he reminded himself. Then he shook his head. He believed her. And it was good to see that they weren't trying to sweep the incident under the rug.

Leaning back and rolling his neck to ease the strain, he realized he'd been at it for nearly two hours. He glanced over at the bed. Myra had turned, her hand lying on the spot he'd been occupying, as if she'd searched for him. His gut twisted and he got up, quietly made his way to the fridge and opened a beer.

He took a long pull while considering his options. Show the information he'd gathered to Myra, Michael and Linda, work with them to solve the problem. He had no doubt, based on what Myra had told him of Arizona, that if the trouble had been caused by wolves, she would handle it. But when the source was human? Piece-of-shit ranchers who wanted a piece of the public land pie? He wasn't sure what she would do, let alone how she would react to his methods of gathering evidence.

One more drink nearly drained the bottle. He rolled the cold glass over his forehead. Did he want to make friends or enemies? Or go back to being a hermit, living his life isolated from the dramas that other people invariably provided. He finished the beer, put it on the counter and walked silently to the bed.

His fingers itched to move her hair back from her face, his body pulsed with the need to lay down, wake her up with slow loving, finish her off with hard fucking.

His heart did that stupid twisty thing again and his decision was made. He took one step back, then another, turned and dressed. The door made only the smallest of sounds when he closed it behind him and headed out.

IT ONLY TOOK a few hours to accomplish, and most of that was spent driving to where he needed to go. Though it was several ranchers who'd banded together, there were two definite leaders. Unsurprisingly, they were the two biggest assholes, and therefore it hadn't been difficult to dig up compromising information on both of them. Info they wouldn't want shared with the world.

Blackmail might be a dirty word to some, but he considered it just when turned against those who'd hatched a plan to poison wolves and get the community angry enough to lift the hunting and land restrictions on the public forest.

When he walked up to the cabin, Myra was sitting on the porch, curled up with a book on the Adirondack chair, the last light of the day bathing her in a warm glow. She gave him a tentative smile as he approached, leaned against the rail next to her.

"I did some digging. Figured out they were dropping poisoned meat into the public land portion of the forest, trying to make the wolves sick enough to attack the humans. They had ranchers and hunters ready to rally the town as soon as they could get a wolf or two to attack. Of course, they don't know there are werewolves running those woods, stopping the wolves before they could cause real trouble."

She blinked at him. "I see. How were you able to find out all of this? Do you have proof we can take to the police?"

He handed her a thumb drive. "Everything is on here. No need to go to the police, I've handled it. You'll see some information on there about the top two guys. In case I'm not around, that's what you can use to keep them in line. Believe me, they're motivated to get with the program and back off the wolves."

She stared at the drive. "You found information about them on the computer. Figured out who they were online."

"Basically."

She looked back at the cabin. "Is that how you make your living? Hacking and blackmailing?"

He didn't have to answer. Owed her nothing, as far as he was concerned. But maybe if she knew who he was, the person he needed to be after what was done to him, she'd feel better about walking away, leaving him be.

"Blackmail isn't the right word. Stealing is probably the right word."

Her eyes opened wide.

"From drug dealers, mostly. You'd be amazed how many have shitty internet security. But truthfully, I don't need much." He gestured at the cabin. "I just want to live here, do my thing, be at peace in my woods. This has been interesting, meeting you all, getting to know what you're about. I'm glad to know you took care of Arizona, I should have done something about that years ago. It's on me that I didn't."

Her mouth opened and closed a few times as she formulated a response. "I see," she finally said. "How come you didn't tell me about what you'd found?"

"You were sleeping." The lameness of the response was not lost on him, but she merely nodded.

She stood, reached a hand out to him, stopped when he moved to the side.

"Okay. Right." She sighed. "Adam, you don't have to join the pack to be a part of our world. There's even an online community you might like to check out. I want you to understand you have a place, you're not alone."

"I like my place. I'm happy here." That he was angry and defensive irritated him, so he took a deep breath. "If I want to get more touchy-feely with the wolves, I know where to go."

She nodded. "Okay. I'll head out. I want you to consider going to Idaho. Meet Hillary and Alexis, at Mountain Pack. Alexis doesn't have any real family left, so they took her in and are working on an official adoption. See that they're both happy, and that their lives are really, really good. They're not just…existing."

He wasn't sure what expression showed on his face but she gave him a sad smile and continued. "I want to challenge you to *live*. Not to just exist by scrounging off the bottom feeders, but to experience joy and happiness. I hope you'll contact me, let me know you've visited Hillary, how you're faring. But mostly I just hope you start living again. Don't let him continue to ruin your life."

She acted quickly, while a dozen possible responses moved through his head, to kiss him on the lips. Then she was gone. Striding into the cabin, she was back only a minute later with her bag and keys in hand. She gave him a nod and walked to the truck.

He stood still, watching as the truck backed up, turned around. Watching the dust trail as it bloomed, then slowly dissipated. Watched as the sun set and the noises of the forest intruded on his attempt to not think. To not wonder about what could be or what might have been. When the evening breeze began to pick up, he shivered and walked inside.

Ten days later

Adam gave himself a bit of a shake as he came off the plane. He didn't particularly enjoy being cooped up in a metal tube, even if it was a short flight. Maybe he'd made the wrong decision in not driving out, but once he'd decided to meet Mountain Pack, he'd figured he'd better do it right away or he'd just forget about it entirely. If he started driving, he couldn't be sure he'd end up at the intended destination.

His initial call to Hillary Jenner had been easier than he'd thought. She'd encouraged him to come visit, see for himself that she and Alexis were well. He was pretty sure she'd heard his whole story from Myra, but she sounded eager to meet him. He told himself he was doing it for her and the girl. Maybe that was mostly true. Maybe.

He hitched his backpack up on his shoulder and made his way quickly through the small airport. Somehow he knew the couple standing in front of the SUV was Hillary and Zach. Zach stood up away from the truck as he approached.

They did the strength-measuring thing, and he was interested to find that they were equals. Although, after Myra's stories, it shouldn't have been a surprise. He offered his hand to Hillary.

"Adam Thorpe."

"I'm Hillary Jenner." She took his hand for a beat, then pulled him in for a hug.

It was the most contact he'd had with anyone since he'd sent Myra on her way. It felt good. Damn it. He pulled away, turned to her husband, who offered his hand.

"Zach. It's good to meet you."

"Likewise."

"You want to stop for food on the way in? It's a little early for lunch, but it's about an hour drive to the house," Jenner told him.

Yeah, he'd made the wrong choice, should have just driven himself to their place. Live and learn.

"I could eat." he'd fully regained his appetite after being sick, though he hadn't quite managed to get rid of an edgy restlessness. He figured once he'd gotten this obligation out of the way, he could go back to the way things had been. Hoped.

They took their seats at a steak restaurant not far from the airport and ordered, keeping the conversation light in the packed room. He'd looked them both up online, of course.

"You're a woodworker?" he asked Hillary when the waitress had left.

She smiled. "That's right. I have my own shop."

"She's amazing," Zach chimed in, taking his wife's hand and

kissing her knuckles, a gesture they both seemed mostly unaware of, though she leaned into him more. "Not just at building the stuff, but figuring out what a person wants and designing it so that it turns out even better than they'd imagined."

"That sounds like a difficult task," he acknowledged.

She laughed. "Sometimes yes, sometimes not so much. I'm just glad I figured out a way to earn a living without working for anyone else, and actually enjoy myself."

He nodded. "I'm guessing most alphas don't make the greatest employees.

Zach raised the soda the waiter had just brought him in agreement.

"What about you?" Hillary asked.

"I do computer stuff. I live very simply, so I don't need much."

"Myra said you were out there on your own. I know what that's like, keeping your distance from the other wolves." She'd lowered her voice but glanced around their table. "But you still need people in your life."

"Did you?"

"I had friends, an employee I was close to. It helped."

Probably judging his comfort level with the conversation, she quickly changed tactics.

"If you'd told me a year ago I'd be surrounded by so many people, so many friends and family, and that I'd actually like it, I would have called you crazy. We don't live in the pack house, so we do have our privacy when we need it, but there's always someone who wants to talk, needs advice, wants to share something, or just needs a hug. It's…" She looked at her husband. "Amazing."

Zach smiled and met Adam's eyes. "Sorry, we're still in the honeymoon phase."

"From what I hear, we'll get worse, not better," Hillary laughed.

Zach grinned. "No comment."

"Ha. Well, no complaints on this end, at least not so far."

Adam watched with some amusement as Zach playfully growled at Hillary and she batted him away. She looked over at him, cleared her throat. "Um. Sorry. Again. Anyway, as I was saying, my life has changed in so many ways, but I don't regret a single thing." She shook her head. "But that's not what I meant to go on about, either. Tell me about you. About your cabin in the woods."

"Not much to tell." He sat back as the waiter put a plate in front of him. "Like I said, I live a simple life. Books and my computer, running in the woods." He shrugged, ate a couple of bites. "I wouldn't exactly say I'm a hermit, though I suppose it's a close thing. The cabin in Montana is the longest I've settled in somewhere. Before that I moved around a lot, exploring the country, even Canada for a time."

Hillary took a drink of her soda, pointed the glass at him. "You get around. Think you'll stay in Montana now or get itchy feet again?"

He thought about it. He'd been there a couple of years now. He liked the woods well enough, the town well enough, but it was just a place to be for him. He didn't love it. Didn't need it. He just needed a place that was his. "I don't have any plans to move right now, but I guess I don't see myself staying there forever, either."

"Hmm," was Hillary's response.

Zach laughed. "Uh oh, Larry's getting ideas. Better watch yourself."

"Oh, shut up. I was just wondering what type of women, or men, you like. We have some great single wolves in the pack that I've been getting to know."

He choked on his drink—and interestingly enough, so did Zach.

"Uh. Baby. None of the unmated wolves are near close enough in power for this guy."

"So, it's not all about being mates." She laughed at the outraged look on her husband's face. "Not until you actually meet your mate. You had relationships before we met."

"Okay, but what makes you a matchmaker all of a sudden?"

"Hey, aren't Stee and Alex deliriously happy?" She looked at Adam. "My employee, the one I mentioned before, turned out to be mates with Zach's second."

"I don't know that you can take credit for matchmaking there when you just happened to be the one who introduced them, and they were mates."

She stuck her tongue out at him and returned her attention to Adam.

"I'm perfectly capable of finding my own women, thank you very much. Besides, would you really want another alpha wolf in your territory?"

"Wouldn't bother me as long as you're not an asshole. But you're right, you'd do better with your own territory, your own pack. You're clearly meant to be an alpha. We need to find out who all the single alpha ladies are out there so you can go check them out."

"Taking care of other wolves is not high on my agenda." And he certainly didn't need any other alpha females getting under his skin. He was having a hard enough time getting the scent and feel and look of one particular one out of his head.

"Hmm," she repeated.

They returned to the SUV and headed out. The couple told him about their land, part of it pack land, part of it Jenner land, part of it public land. They drove through a town bigger than the one he currently called home, then another twenty minutes until Zach turned down a road marked "Private Property." It was still a couple of miles farther before they reached a security gate that Zach coded them through.

"You all have much trouble out this way?" he asked.

"Nope, but we do what we can to keep it that way. We're way proactive on that, my second is a security expert, so I let him do his thing."

Adam couldn't argue the logic on that.

When they spotted the house, he was a bit surprised. Zach hadn't seemed like a particularly rich guy, but the house was huge. He supposed being an alpha might require a bit more space to entertain and host than his cabin in the woods. Putting a loner wolf like himself up for a couple of nights, for example.

He dumped his pack in the room Hillary showed him, then

followed her back down the stairs, past a living room that looked like no one used it and into a den that looked well lived in. He took a seat on the leather couch at Hillary's indication. She sat on the other end, curled her leg under her and faced him as Zach came in, handed him a beer, and took a seat in a lounge chair.

"Tell me," Hillary said.

He examined her over his beer as he took a drink. He'd come here to check on her, make sure she and the girl were good. The evidence was pretty clear that she was more than good. And it was obvious to him that she had invited him here to make the same judgement on him. Probably she wasn't so easily convinced on his state of well-being.

Still, there was nothing that obligated him to open up. And yet, his reticence seemed more habit than actual reluctance to talk to her. He couldn't deny that he felt a connection, a sense of rightness that she was happy. That was unexpected. He'd really just hoped to not feel too guilty.

He took another drink while she watched him patiently. Glancing at Zach, he saw only amused understanding.

"You know about Arizona. Nothing much to say about that. I got shot, I made it out, I stayed low, kept to myself. Ended up in Montana. I knew where the local pack was, watched them enough to know they weren't up to anything bad, stayed out of their way until these shitheads decided that poisoning the wolves to create trouble in town and get themselves a license to kill was a good idea."

"And you met Myra," Hillary said after a moment.

He could see that she'd heard the story, figured there was no use pretending otherwise. "Yeah, I'm not gonna lie, it was a shock to have someone put me down like that. I don't love knowing that there are people out there that can still do that to me. Even though it was necessary, and a good thing she was there." He cleared his throat, drank more beer.

"Hmph." Hillary set her drink down on an end table and pulled her other leg in front of her so that she could face him fully. "You do know that according to Myra and Michael both, the very fact that you hesitated, didn't attack them right away, was a pretty amazing bit of strength on your part. If you'd met up with a human or a weaker wolf, instead of them, you likely would have scared them away."

A little ball of sickness that had been sitting in his gut, mostly unnoticed, dissolved. "Maybe."

She nodded. "Likely. But they couldn't take that chance, so Myra stopped you."

He nodded. "She was right to do it."

"And you do know," Zach chimed in, "that Myra didn't stop you just on her own. She had to draw on power from some other alphas. From us. She needed to go hard and fast because she couldn't sustain that draw from us for long. Or at least, we don't think so, it's not something that's happened in our generation, and not something we want to play around with or test."

He sat back. He hadn't known that. It should have made him feel better. Did, a bit. But it also made him even more grateful that it had been Myra to find him in the woods that day.

"Is that something you guys do, too? Draw power from your pack?"

"We can. Again, it's rare." Zach paused, seemed to consider his words. "You're probably aware that physical challenges for position are also rare in packs. But it does happen on occasion. I don't think the power draw would work in that situation. I don't know if it's the magic that stops it, or the collective will of the pack, or the stubborn will of the alpha. I don't know, I just know, instinctively, that I wouldn't even try, but if for some reason I did, it wouldn't work. The bond is most usually used in the other direction."

Adam frowned, not sure he understood. "You send power to your wolves?"

Hillary chimed in. "Sometimes. Usually it's like sending a burst of strength to a wolf that needs help changing, because they're sick, or exhausted. Or sending comfort, or even love, to a pack member that needs it."

He sort of understood. But not really. If he thought about it, which he tried not to, he could identify a little piece of himself that was connected to Myra. He could imagine sending something along that piece, back to her. Wasn't particularly comfortable with that thought, especially if he considered that it was reciprocal.

Finishing off his drink, he set the bottle on the table next to him. "Good to know."

"Actually, that reminds me of something," Zach said, looking at Hillary. "In a couple of days, Myra will hand the National Presidency over to Marco Hernandez, in Elk Ridge."

Hillary's eyebrows drew together. "Where's Elk Ridge?"

"Northern California. The reason I mention it is that you might feel something, during the transfer. Maybe not, since you don't know Marco, but I do, so you might get some echo through that, as well as your friendship with Myra." He looked to Adam. "You might get something too, so just be aware."

Great. He was trying to forget the woman, but she just wasn't cooperating with that, at all.

CHAPTER SIX

Myra wasn't sure how forgettable she was or wasn't, but she was sure having a hard time forgetting Adam. Her body was reminding her of him constantly, sending her flashes of memory along with warm pulses of need. His hands on her hips, his lips on hers, his growling voice in her ear. All of them served to make her wet, make her skin tingle in need, make her lose track of what she should be doing, instead of thinking of that sexy loner wolf.

She'd returned to St. Louis only days after having left her pack, and yet part of her felt like she was a whole new wolf. She'd tried to shake the feeling, but everything just felt...off. Her firsts, Kendra and Deacon, had kept things moving smoothly. The idea that they didn't even need her at all was pathetic and she pushed it aside. One of the reasons she made a good National President was that if she actually needed to act, as she had this time, she could comfortably do what was necessary without a single worry about her own pack's needs.

It had been ten days, and she still didn't feel like she had before she'd left. She felt like she was just a visitor in her own life, somehow.

Her father gave her a hip check, and she nipped at him playfully. Leave it to Dad to snap her out of her brain and remind her that she was part of a pack. She looked around her. Her wolves ranged through the woods, Dario scratching his back against a tree, Alisha bowing down in front of him to entice him to play. They'd decided to go for a long run together, those who weren't stuck at work, to enjoy a beautiful, sunny morning after a week of rain and gray.

It was a decent-size group and they'd run far before coming to a rest near a creek. A creek that Zavi was about to push Kyle into, if he didn't watch himself. But Kyle wasn't fourth for nothing, and just as Zavi was about to connect, he stepped out of the way and she splashed into the creek, scrabbling but unable to stop herself.

Her father huffed in amusement. Frank and her mother had retired as firsts three years ago, but he was still her most trusted advisor. Kendra and Deacon, once mated, had surged in power, and her parents took the opportunity to slow down in life. Rosa, her mom, preferred to mother the younger wolves and leave the rest of pack business to the new hierarchy.

They made their way back to the pack house, in no particular hurry. She raced Kendra for a while, enjoying the warm air against her fur, the pure joy of speeding through the forest, at peace with the land. When they arrived back, some of the wolves simply curled up in the den to sleep, while others turned off to go to their own homes, or turned back to their human selves so they could drive home.

She turned and dressed, chatting with Alisha as she walked out to the cars. Her parents were standing next to her dad's beat-up sedan.

"Why don't you come back with us, have some lunch," her mom suggested.

They'd eaten a huge breakfast before heading out for the run, but of course, she was starving. Knowing her mom, there'd be a roast in the slow cooker, timed perfectly for their arrival.

"Sounds great, Mom, I'll meet you there." She kissed Rosa's cheek and followed behind them in her not-so-beat-up sedan. Using the hands-free on her phone, she texted her best friend, Cindy, who was still at work, and made plans to get together the next day. She pulled up to the house she'd grown up in and finally felt at home again.

When they'd eaten half the roast and a boatload of potatoes, Frank wiped his mouth with his napkin and looked at her.

"Feeling like you're all set to hand over the presidency?"

She waggled her hand. "Mostly. I've had inquiries from some hierarchy wolves around the country interested in going to Arizona. But so far, none that I think are strong enough to be alpha there. A couple who might be strong enough to take over an established pack, but none I would trust in this situation."

Her mother nodded. "Even if you don't bring any of the Mesa Pack wolves back, it's tricky to start a new pack from scratch."

"Exactly. I for sure wouldn't let any of the rogue Phoenix Pack back, but there are some of the Mesa Pack that would like to go home, and that requires care."

"Have you put out a call for alphas?" Frank asked.

"No, I figured if the right person, or pair, doesn't come to the forefront before I leave, I'll let Marco handle it, since he'll be the president needing to monitor and deal with the new pack."

"Seems fair," Rosa agreed.

"It's a hell of a thing," Frank said.

"I know, it's still hard to comprehend, even though I was there." She shook her head in amazement, still horrified by what she'd learned. She wasn't sure she'd quite come to grips with the whole thing, even now. Maybe that was why she still felt off. Most of the year had gone just as her previous term had several years ago. Uneventful.

"It...sucked," she acknowledged. Though her hierarchy, even her fellow alphas like Zach and Hillary, would understand what she was feeling, at least in theory, she supposed her parents were the only ones she was willing to actually share it with. "The hardest thing I've ever had to do, hopefully *will* ever have to do. Judging each of those wolves, deciding who had to die, who could go to a pack they had relatives in, who needed to go to a stronger pack, capable of keeping an eye on them, but also helping them to get back to a healthy place. I never thought I'd have to determine so many fates."

Frank reached out, put his hand on hers. "No one doubts that you made the right decisions. No one questions the choices that you made."

Rosa looked at her with a mother's eyes, full of sympathy and pain at the idea that her baby might be hurting. "Do you? Question your decisions," she asked softly.

She gave Rosa a watery smile. "No, I'm good on that part. It sucked, but I'm not second-guessing myself."

Satisfied, Rosa nodded. "That's my girl."

"What about this guy out in Montana?" Frank asked.

"Adam," she said, reaching for her water. "He'll be okay. I just wish he could be..." She shook her head. "I wish he could be better than okay, but I don't see that happening if he refuses to join our world more fully."

She took a drink, then looked at them when they remained silent. "What?"

"You just look sad," her mom said.

"Well, I am, I guess. I hate that something so awful happened to him and that he's not living as good a life as he could be. But he has no reason to believe me that it would be better. I can't force him into it."

"He'll find his way," Rosa assured her. "Speaking of finding their way, did I tell you that your cousin Ashley met her mate while on vacation in Rome?"

"What? No! An Italian wolf? Or man?"

"A wolf. From Florida."

She laughed. "That's awesome. Have they figured out who's moving where?"

"Not yet, but that reminds me. Your father and I are thinking of selling this house. Getting something smaller."

Stunned, Myra sat back. "You're selling the house?"

"We're thinking about it. It's pretty big for just the two of us, especially now that we're not hierarchy. We don't host many visitors anymore."

That was true, but...okay, there was no good but. Her mom was absolutely right. Somehow it just echoed her earlier feelings about not being home.

"That's true. Where are you thinking of moving?"

"We haven't looked into it much, yet, just wanted to let you know it was an idea."

"It makes sense. It's just sort of a shock."

Her dad leaned over and kissed her temple. "No matter where we go, you always have a place with us."

Her nose tingled, a sure sign she was getting emotional and a bit teary. "I know, Dad. Thanks." Her parents' unwavering love and support had been a huge part of her recovery when Eric died. Knowing that her pain hurt them had helped her to ease her way clear of the stultifying grief. She'd moved in with them for a year and had appreciated their willingness to let her grieve, even as they hoped she'd move past it.

The peace she'd finally managed to gain on the run with her pack was fading. She finished her water and stood. "Thanks for lunch. I better get home."

She could see the surprise on their faces but she was becoming too antsy to sit for any longer. "I love you guys, I'll see you tomorrow."

As she drove home, she felt needy, almost itchy. Like she needed to pull out her vibrator and see about recreating all the good things she'd experienced in bed with Adam. And there were a lot of good things.

The drive to her house was pretty quick. She decided to take a bath, see if that would help. Then maybe she could settle down, get some paperwork done, and cook herself a nice dinner. She did the whole ritual, lighting candles, pouring an expensive bubble bath—a gift from her best friend—pulled her little bath pillow out from under the sink, hung a silk robe on the back of the door, and slid into the warm water.

It felt wonderful, and she determinedly relaxed all the muscles in her body. She closed her eyes, breathed in the soothing lavender, and tried to relax.

Tried. Thoughts of Adam intruded immediately. To say she'd enjoyed their playtime together was an understatement. While she'd been with a few men in the years since Eric's death, even had minor relationships, she hadn't truly connected with any of them. It just wasn't possible, when you'd been mated, to feel much satisfaction in something that was so...much less.

Adam had been different, though. While it still didn't compare to a mating bond, it was much more powerful than she'd realized, if she was obsessing about him ten days later.

She wondered if she should call him. She'd talked to Hillary, knew that Adam had spoken to her, and agreed to go to Mountain View for a visit. The fact had relieved her a bit. She took in a breath, relaxed a bit more. Yes, after he visited Mountain View, maybe he'd be in a better place, emotionally. Realize that there was no guilt for him to feel about how he'd left Arizona behind and focused on making a new life for himself. And seeing a healthy pack in action, up close and personal, instead of the distance he kept from Bitterroot, that might help as well.

Then, maybe he'd be open to a relationship. Long distance might actually suit him and his need to be alone at times.

She watched the play of candlelight on the bubbles, swirled a finger through them until she'd cleared a delicate path to one of her nipples. It stood at semi-attention, so she idly circled it, not quite touching, circling and circling as it grew more and more taught. She ached to feel a touch there, but it wasn't her finger she wanted. It was his. She repeated the pattern over her other breast, but then couldn't stand the need anymore and tweaked both nipples. She nearly cried out at the sensation, imagined it was larger, rougher fingers working the points. She dipped her hands in the water, then dribbled big drops over her breasts. It wasn't enough.

The hot water made her face slick, but the burning need was more than that. She needed him. Closing her eyes, she thought of his hands, his warmth, his strength. She imagined it was his hand gliding through the water, along her stomach until it cupped her pussy. His fingers that rubbed gently, too gently, over her clit, while the other hand pulled at her nipple. His warm breath heating her face, her neck, his heartbeat that seemed to echo through her ears.

She eased two fingers into herself, the palm of her hand pressing hard circles onto that bundle of nerves that pulsed with need. Her feet pushed hard against the end of the tub, her neck arching hard into the pillow, as her hips rose, chasing her teasing fingers. His fingers. Rough and long, she imagined them pushing deep, adding a third. In her mind, she pictured his face, close to hers, his eyes boring into hers, heard his voice. *Come for me.*

And she did. Hard. With a cry and a slosh of water over the side of the tub, she slammed back down, panting.

Her eyes popped open wide. Holy shit, she'd actually felt him at the end there. Had connected with him. Shit. She hadn't meant to, couldn't believe she'd done it so easily, so unconsciously. Now she'd have to apologize for invading his privacy, forcing her emotions through to him, via a link she hadn't realize was that strong.

Would he be pissed? Panicked that if she could do that, she might be able to do something bad? She pulled the drain, blew out the candles and quickly dried herself off. She didn't even bother with the robe, just moved to her bedroom where she'd left her cell phone and started a message to him. Shit, that was being cowardly.

Before she could stress about it anymore, she pressed the link to call him.

"Myra." The growl in his voice sent shivers through her, almost like an aftershock.

"Adam. I'm so sorry, I didn't mean for that to happen. I hope you can believe me."

She waited, six agonizing heartbeats, before he answered.

"I know. I believe you."

Her breath exploded out of her and she sat down hard on the bed. "Okay. Well. I just wanted to let you know."

"Are you all right?"

"Me? Yeah, sure. Sure." She smacked her forehead. "You? How is it going at Hillary and Zach's?"

"Fine. I've only been here a couple of hours, but…it's good. It's not as…annoying as I thought it'd be."

Relief sang through her. "I knew you'd like them, if you gave them a chance."

"Yeah, well. Thanks for calling."

"Right. Okay." She swallowed around the lump that had suddenly ballooned in her throat. "Goodbye, Adam."

"Goodbye, Myra."

She pressed the screen to hang up and let the phone slide out of her hands onto the bed. And cried.

ADAM WAS man enough to admit that he was scared. He'd been in some tough situations in his life, but he was hard-pressed to think of one that had been more unnerving than having an eight-year-old girl staring into his eyes as if she could read every transgression and sin on his soul.

He refused to squirm, met her gaze, and waited for judgment.

She silently held her hand out to him. Not exactly sure of himself, he took the little hand into his and gave it a gentle shake.

Alexis broke out into a huge grin. "You're nice," she declared.

"Well, thank you. You seem pretty nice yourself."

She sat down on the couch they were standing in front of. The seat next to the one he'd been on when she and Tracy, Zach's sister-in-law, had come home from school. Hillary had brought him here to Zach's brother, Aaron's, house, so that he could meet Alexis. Hillary now held a squirming bundle of boy he'd been told was Ryder, and she shot him a grin but continued whatever conversation she'd started up with her friend, leaving him to his own devices.

"You like it here?" he asked, figuring he might as well cut to the chase.

She nodded.

"Well, that's good. They treat you nicely?"

She smiled, nodded again. Ryder shouted "Lesis" and Adam watched as Hillary managed to get him to the floor before he launched himself airborne to the couch. The kid made a beeline for them and Alexis giggled. The part of himself that had been reserving judgment on all of these wolves dissolved. He knew it had only been a couple of weeks since the girl had been rescued from an awful situation, and he knew kids were resilient, but he had to take this as evidence that these were good people.

The boy pulled himself up to standing by clutching at Adam's jeans. When Alexis started to reach down, Adam forced himself to do it instead, plopping the wiggling toddler into her lap for her.

"Lesis!" Ryder pressed his face into her body. Alexis answered by bending down to give him kisses.

He realized the ladies had stopped talking, looked to find them watching the scene with suspiciously watery eyes. Yeah, these were good people.

The front door opened and Alexis attempted to get off the couch, so Adam gave her a little help, but as soon as she was on her feet, she took the kid to his father, who scooped them both up into a bear hug.

Adam stood and gave a nod to the man as he approached. Aaron bent his head a bit to show submission. The wolf inside Adam approved. The man himself was uncomfortable, since he was currently in this guy's home. Aaron seemed completely unconcerned.

"I'm going to change out of these clothes and then it's my turn to make dinner tonight. Who's going to help me?" Aaron asked.

"Me," Alexis said, laying her head on Aaron's shoulder. Ryder raised both hands in the air in agreement. Tracy moved to greet her husband, who put the kids down, cupped her face in his hands and did a proper job of kissing her hello.

Before long, Adam found himself helping Alexis tear up lettuce for the salad.

"You were the one who volunteered for kitchen duty, not me," he teased.

She turned solemn eyes to his, but he saw the twinkle. "You don't want to help?"

"Ah, I guess it's okay," he admitted.

Hillary was chopping carrots at the other end of the table. "You have to watch this one." She gestured to Alexis. "She has amazing powers of persuasion with just a single look."

Alexis giggled.

"As long as she only uses her powers for good, I guess we're safe enough."

Hillary winked at him. Tracy walked up and handed out glasses of wine. "We may put you to work, but we'll pay you with beverages, a good meal, and excellent company."

"That's a deal I can get behind." And surprisingly, he meant it. He wasn't feeling at all cooped up or surrounded, though he'd not had this much interaction with this many people in…well, who the fuck knew how long.

"Zach's on his way. He was wondering if you wanted to go to the bar tonight, play some pool. I can't, I need to work on a design I promised to rush."

"Sure."

Tracy sat down next to him. "If you don't want to talk about it, I understand, but I've been wondering about your family. From before. You never went back to Arizona?"

He side-eyed the kid but figured she knew enough about unhappy shit to not get upset over a bit of reality, but he had to clean up his internal language a bit.

"My parents were conservative idiots. Overly religious, to my mind. My brother was gay, and while it wasn't until he graduated high school that he came out, we'd known for some time that they wouldn't approve. He turned eighteen while I was a sophomore in college and told them. As expected, they lost their minds. He moved in with me, we dropped contact with my parents and their families. There might be some relatives out there that aren't jerks, but we didn't really know them because they weren't the type my parents kept in touch with."

Alexis scooted over in her chair so that she could rest her head on his arm. The sudden lump in his throat was a surprise. He ripped more lettuce for a second.

"He'd never been the healthiest kid, and he died three months before he would have graduated from college, from complications with his asthma."

"How terrible, I'm so sorry I brought it up."

He heard the distress in her voice, so managed to work up a smile for her. "It's okay. Actually, it's kind of nice. I haven't spoken about him in a very long time. I don't want to think he's been forgotten by the world."

"What was his name?" Hillary asked.

He had to swallow around that damn lump. "James. Jamey."

"I bet we would have liked him. He would have thought you were badass as a wolf."

He gave a bark of laughter. "Yeah, I guess he would have. And you definitely would have liked him. He was a great guy."

Aaron chose that moment to come to the table with a platter of chicken thighs and a giant bowl of mashed potatoes. "Are you all really still working on that salad?"

Adam looked down to see he'd pretty much torn up the last of the lettuce. Alexis held the bowl for him and he dumped the pieces in. Hillary slid over her plate of cut-up carrots and he added those. There was already avocado and croutons, so they called it complete as the sound of Zach entering the house reached them.

Dinner with a two-year-old was a new experience for Adam, but not an unpleasant one. He found that, as Hillary had warned him, Alexis didn't speak often, but she payed attention to everything that was going on around her. And she was, unquestionably, happy to be there. So was Hillary, and not just because of her husband. She was clearly an everyday part of this family, of the pack, even though she hadn't been here long, either.

Dessert was a bowl of mint chip ice cream, another thing he

couldn't remember the last time he'd experienced. Myra's comments about the lack of life he was actually living intruded, but luckily he had plans to play pool to distract him. At least he could remember the last time he'd played, though now that he thought about it, five years wasn't exactly an endorsement to his claims of living much of a life.

He followed Zach into the bar that the pack owned.

"If any humans had shown up and not yet been maneuvered out, one of the waitstaff would be at the door, playing bouncer, to let us know. Since no one is watching the door, we can talk freely."

He nodded. "Good to know. I didn't know places like this existed."

"Some of the bigger packs have them, depending on the size of the towns they live in, how far off the beaten track they are."

"Seems like Mountain Pack is pretty large for being so far from any major city."

"Yeah, we like that, but some find it easier to get work and raise families in the city. Can't blame them, sometimes it's hard to make sure all of my wolves are able to work full-time jobs if they want them, but we're big enough to provide a lot of the jobs ourselves."

A man with blond hair to his shoulders and a shirt with the name of the bar on it walked up to them. "Zach, it's been a while. Letting married life cramp your style?"

Zachary laughed hard. "Yeah, that's exactly right. Peter, this is a friend from out of town, Adam Thorpe. Adam, our third, and my cousin, Peter Jenner."

Peter lowered his head for a second, then offered his hand. Adam shook it, taking a look around. "This is a nice place. You work here?"

"I'm the manager. You guys want a table? Or straight to pool?"

Zach clapped him on the back. "We'll get a game started. You have time to play a round?"

"Sure. Theo's back there taking some practice shots, waiting for an interesting game."

Zach snorted. "Not sure we can promise that, but we'll give it a go." He pointed to the pool table farthest away and the large man working it. "Theo paid his way through college hustling pool, or so the rumors go."

"I prefer the rumor that he was a gigolo," Peter said as he signaled a waiter to bring them beers.

Laughing, Zach led them to the man in question, who, Adam discovered as they began to play, was indeed good enough to have been a hustler. Adam and Zach lost the first round, though not necessarily as badly as they could have. Peter was an okay player, Adam was a bit better, Zach was good, Theo was great. But they had a good time and he only thought about Myra and what had happened every other minute, instead of constantly. Should he check up on her, make sure she was all right? She'd been distressed by what had happened.

He gave Peter a good-natured jab to the shoulder when the other man scratched, took his time placing the cue ball and selecting his shot. A woman wandered by, stood chatting with Peter, angling herself in such a way that Adam couldn't miss what she had on display. He blocked her from his mind and took the shot, pleased with the result. When he moved around the table for his next move, she casually shifted over to conversation with Zach so that she was still in his line of sight.

Again, he ignored her and made the shot. It was a trickier move, the only one available that he could see, and he actually almost made it, but not quite. He gave Zach a shrug.

"It's cool, I'm sure we'll run them off the table next time," Zach said, laughing. "Let me introduce you to Michelle. She's just come home from college for a long weekend."

The woman, who he had to try hard not to think of as a girl—fuck, he was getting old—managed to be both sultry and submissive at the same time. While he found her red hair and amber eyes, well-displayed full figure, and direct but respectful gaze attractive, he was mostly unnerved. She was nearly twenty years younger than him. Christ, he really *was* getting old.

He chatted long enough to be polite, then moved back to the

table, pretending more interest in Theo's next shot than he actually felt. The other man gave him a knowing look, but Adam was pretty sure there was a shit-eating grin lurking behind the solemn facade.

When he turned back to find his beer, Michelle picked it up, handed it to him with one hand while running her other up his arm. "How long are you going to be in Mountain View?" she asked.

He couldn't keep from shrugging off her hand, even if it would have been polite. His reaction was almost visceral, and while he held back the growl that would have been overreaction, he wasn't cool with her touching him—and she knew it. She took a small step back, dropping her hand and her gaze, biting her lip.

Shit. He didn't want to be an asshole. "School, huh? What are you studying?"

She lifted her head, shyer now, crossing her arms over her chest. "Engineering."

They spent the next little while with her excitedly telling him her plans for the future, while he was careful to communicate that his interest was purely friendly. Once she realized that, she became more relaxed, more animated, with Zach joining in the conversation, two elders expressing interest in the future plans of a young one. Fuck. He shook his head at himself as he and Zach lost the second game.

The bar had filled up and all the tables were full. There were sure to be others waiting for a table, so he signaled Zach.

"Ready to head out, or you want to grab a table for another drink?"

"This was nice, but more than enough for a hermit like me."

"Yeah, about that. You're going to ruin that hermit reputation with all this socializing. Got to say, man, you weren't exactly the life of the party, but you weren't sitting in a corner glaring at anyone who dared approach you, either."

"I like doing my thing, living my way. I deal with people on my own terms. Doesn't mean I don't like people."

They walked to the truck and headed back. "You were good with

Michelle back there. Easing her back, redirecting her without stomping on her ego."

"She's a good kid." He snorted.

Zach's laugh was a full one. "Yeah, we're getting old, for sure. The young ones that are going to be strong, they're attracted to the power, on a subconscious level sometimes."

"You don't think it was my manly good looks and incredible charm?"

Zach's snort was answer enough, and Adam smiled as he looked out the window and considered where his life had turned. Things had changed in the last week, but he couldn't say he minded any of it. And now that he wasn't surrounded by kids and strangers, he let the thoughts of Myra that hadn't ever quite gone away, push forward. The phone call with her had been tough, mostly because he'd still been recovering from the assault of sensation that had seemed to come from nowhere. He'd been putting his things away, about to head out with Hillary to go meet Alexis and Tracy, when the heat and need and want had hit him. He'd gone hard and had to work to hold back his release as he'd felt Myra achieve hers.

Then his phone had buzzed and he'd known it was her. She'd sounded worried, not the reaction he's expected considering she'd clearly just had an orgasm. Obviously she'd realized that she'd somehow connected with him and was concerned he'd have a freak-out. Maybe he should have, but he'd still been struggling to ease the throbbing in his system and keep from coming like an adolescent in his jeans. He'd rushed her off the phone and tried to push her out of his mind while meeting the kid and her family, then at the bar. Now he kind of felt like an ass.

"You doing okay, here?" Zach asked.

"Here?"

"Well, with that whole hermit thing. We pushing you on other people too much?"

"I'll tell you no when there's something I don't want to do. Mommy."

Zach grinned at him. "Hey, I'm a kind and sensitive alpha, my wife says so."

"Yeah, well, she's still in the honeymoon phase. Which is a neat trick, since my understanding is you haven't even taken her on a honeymoon."

"It's in the works, man. With a mate, things happen fast. But it takes time to plan a stellar honeymoon. And I'm not giving her anything less than stellar."

"You're liking this whole mate thing. You've been looking forward to it your whole life, I guess?"

Zach tapped his fingers on the wheel as he drove and considered his answer. He glanced over at Adam and nodded. "It's hard not to, when you grow up seeing how amazing it is for two people to be so much a part of each other. I see human couples in love, and it's great, don't get me wrong, but there's so much potential for disaster, and it's awful. With mates, you just don't have those misunderstandings, or the change in feelings. You don't grow apart, because you're growing together not just in each other's company, but as part of each other's souls."

"Deep, man."

Zach laughed. "The other night, Hillary had to get up early and I was doing some paperwork, so she went to bed before I did. When I went into the bedroom, I was surprised she was on my side of the bed. I figured maybe she was doing something corny like wanting to sleep where my smell was stronger or something like that. I went into the bathroom, trying to be all quiet like, and when I came back, she'd moved to her side."

He slowed for the turn to his house and shot a grin at Adam. "So I get in, and it's nice and warm in there, and she snuggles right up to me. Our legs tangle, like they do, you know, and one of my feet hits her side of the bed, where it's cold. And it hit me. She'd done that to warm up my side of the bed. Now, I'm not saying human couples don't do that kind of thing. I'm just saying it's more natural, more instinctive, with mates. It's just...more. And it's awesome."

"Can't argue with that, I guess. I just haven't been up close to wolves enough to have seen it in action before. But you guys, your brother and his wife. It all seems so intense."

"Yeah. But not in bad way."

They drove up to the house, and he wasn't surprised when Hillary opened the door to greet them before they'd even exited the truck. She walked straight into Zach's arms like they'd been separated for weeks instead of hours.

She gave Adam a hug goodnight, giving him an extra squeeze. "I'm glad you're here."

He nodded. "Me, too. You've got it good out here. I'm happy for that."

Her smile was dazzling. "I really, really do. And I want that for you, too."

He got into bed and thought about his cabin in the woods. From this place, this time, it seemed small and cold and empty. He tried to tell himself that it would all go back to normal when he got home, but he wasn't sure he believed it. Wasn't sure anymore that was what he wanted. Maybe it was time to transition to a new phase in his life. Didn't mean he had to go full-on pack member somewhere. But he could find a better balance than lonely hermit.

Maybe.

He reached out and grabbed his phone without quite knowing he was going to do it. It was late, later in St. Louis. Did she leave her ringer on while she was sleeping? Maybe he could leave her a massage, apologize for earlier. He could probably send her a text message, but he wasn't sure what to say. And there probably wasn't an adequate smiley-face-thingy to say it for him.

Rather than spend more time thinking about it and worrying that he really was regressing to adolescence, he touched her name and heard the phone start to ring.

She answered immediately, but still sounded a little sleepy and breathy. "Adam."

"Hey."

"Hey. You okay?"

"You need to stop worrying about me. I'm not your responsibility."

She didn't answer.

"I called to apologize for earlier. You, uh, caught me off guard and I was getting ready to go meet Alexis and her family, and..."

"No, I'm the one who's sorry. I had no idea that would happen."

He could hear the rustling of sheets, tried very hard not to picture her lying in bed, naked. Body flushed with arousal, licking her lips in anticipation as she—

"I know you're not my responsibility," she said after a moment. "But I'd like to think you're my friend. And I care about how you're doing."

He stared at the ceiling, trying to banish his inner video and concentrate on what she was saying. "Okay. How about you. Glad to be home?"

The silence stretched on a little longer this time, but he waited.

"Mostly. I don't know, everything feels different somehow. I'm starting to wonder if I'm reacting to the Arizona stuff more than I'd realized. I—" She broke off. "I'm sorry, you don't want to hear about that."

"It's fine. Finish."

"Well, I think I did everything right, handled it the way it needed to be handled."

"So, what's the problem then? Anyone telling you otherwise?"

"No, not at all. I just feel...off. Like I'm forgetting something or mishandled something or...I don't know. It's just this vague but nagging feeling I guess."

"You've only been home a week. Maybe you just need to settle in."

"Maybe."

"Will you be glad to be done with the presidency? It's soon, right?"

"A few more days, yeah. I don't know that glad is the right word. Even with the hard things that happened, I'm proud to serve the position. But it's always been for a year, and I'm glad to pass it on to

Marco. Actually, I have to go out west to be there for the transition. I was thinking...are you going to stay in Mountain View a few more days?"

He wasn't sure he wanted this to go where it was leading, but he wasn't sure he wanted to stop it, either.

"Yeah."

"Adam, I'd like to see you again." She said it in a rush and sounded more nervous than he'd ever heard her sound. It was kind of cute. His cock started to harden. He moved a hand down to give it a stroke. It had been unnerving, feeling her emotions, sensations, shooting into him from nowhere. He hadn't liked that he'd had no control over it.

But now he began to get a sense of how it might have been. And how it could be. He concentrated on her voice, on her image in his head. And stroked himself.

"Adam?" Her nerves had gone up, but there was a bit of impatience there, too. Also cute.

"I heard you."

More silence as he stroked his cock and remembered her hand doing it for him, her tongue getting in on the action. He made an effort to send the sensations to her, had no idea if it was working, but he was now fully hard.

He heard her breathing pick up as he remembered the wet heat of her mouth moving on his flesh, her hair brushing over his thighs, her nails digging into his skin.

She gasped. "Are—are you doing that?"

He smiled and let a low, pleased growl issue into the phone.

"Oh my god," she gasped. "You *are* doing that."

His fingers tightened on his shaft and he pumped hard, switching to a memory of him pounding into her, her slick sheath welcoming him, her hips arching to meet him, her hands clinging to his shoulders.

"Adam." It was a low moan this time, and his excellent hearing picked up the wet sounds of her playing with herself, more than a thousand miles away. He growled his approval, closed his eyes and tilted his head back as he imagined her taking everything he had to give.

She came with a soft cry and he followed suit.

After a moment, she spoke, and this time there was amusement in her voice. "So, you wouldn't mind if I came to see you?"

A distant part of himself felt like he was standing on the edge of an abyss. But the more immediate part of him wanted more of what they'd just done, wanted it for real. Wanted to see her face when she talked about Arizona, to make sure she really was good with it, wanted to go to the bar with her so that the other women would know there was no point in approaching him.

Oh shit, he was fucked.

"Come." His response was more gruff and curt than he'd meant, but she seemed to understand.

"Okay, I will." Her soft voice held understanding and promise.

Yeah. Totally fucked.

CHAPTER SEVEN

The next morning, Adam wandered downstairs when he heard activity and smelled coffee. Hillary gave him a warm smile and held out the mug she'd just poured.

"Thanks."

She poured another and took an appreciative drink, then gave him a once over. "Doing okay?"

"The only thing I'm not okay with is how often people keep asking me if I'm doing okay."

She laughed. "All right, I'm done with that now, I promise. I've got some guys coming over today to help me finish setting up the new shop. Moving has been annoying, but I get Zach out of the deal, and now that it's mostly finished, I'm really excited with the new space. You want to come over, or do you have something else in mind?"

He wasn't feeling antsy with all the social activity, but he figured maybe he should be proactive and go for a run on his own *before* getting antsy. "How about I go explore the woods this morning, then come see your place and take you to lunch?"

She smiled. "Good plan. I'll leave my car here for you, catch a ride into town with Zach." She raised her hand when he started to object. "It's easy enough, I promise. I'll feel better knowing you're mobile and not feeling trapped."

"Thanks, I appreciate it."

She wandered away and he took the mug outside to gauge the day. It was a brisk morning, promising to be cool, not cold, which he appreciated. He'd mostly gotten used to the northern climates, but sometimes he missed baking in the Arizona sun. Might be a bitch with fur, though.

He finished his coffee, took the cup back to the kitchen and loaded it into the dishwasher. It felt weird to just strip naked on their porch, so he walked for a bit until he was comfortably surrounded by trees. He found a good branch to tuck his clothes onto and let the wolf take over.

Things were simpler as the wolf. The pleasure of a beautiful day, the joy of running through the woods, chasing small creatures, knowing his place in the scheme of things when he ran across any other animals. It was all so uncomplicated.

He nosed around for a bit, getting a sense of the area, then took off, running where his nose, his instincts, his nature dictated. After an hour or so, he slowed to a stop and found a nice sunny patch. He stretched his body, then lay in the sun and breathed deeply. It was beautiful country up here, not so different from where he'd spent the last three years. His ear twitched to catch a sound now and again but nothing intruded close enough to concern him and he napped easily, enjoying the morning sun.

After a while he rose, stretched again, and loped back in the direction he'd come. He picked up the trail of three werewolves. Of course, there had been scents all over the woods, but this was recent, so he followed until he caught sight of three naked teenagers walking away from him. Amused, he followed for a minute to see if there was a clue what they were up to, but they just trudged along in the general direction of the pack house.

He edged closer until they realized he was there, stopped and turned to look at him. They kept their heads low. He cocked his head in question and one of them cleared his throat.

"We, uh, ran out to the river a ways back. It's not the spot most of the pack uses to swim in on a regular run, it's a farther out, so we could have it to ourselves." He was practically shuffling his feet but he seemed more embarrassed than anxious so Adam just waited. "So we swam for a while, horsed around, you know, and rested. We, uh, well, we thought we'd be able to turn back to wolf and get home, but turns out we weren't strong enough, so we're walking."

He blinked at that. He understood the idea in theory, but had never felt like he couldn't turn when he needed to. These boys were young, though, maybe fifteen, and maybe not going to be particularly powerful, even when grown. He gave a soft woof in understanding and walked closer, rubbing along their legs. Touching gave a better connection and he circled back to sit in front of them. Holding the connection strong in his head, he gave a yip and a nod.

Looking hopeful, the boys each concentrated on themselves, and began to turn. He fed them enough power and energy to make it happen, though he was careful not to overwhelm them with too much. It drained him a bit, but soon enough they were all wolves, setting an easy pace back to civilization, much quicker and safer than walking naked and barefoot through the woods.

He let them lead the way but knew they were on point to hit the pack house when he picked up sounds of a couple of wolves heading toward them. It took a few moments before the boys slowed to a stop and waited for the new wolves to approach. Adam hadn't met any of the pack in wolf form yet, but he was fairly certain the male wolf was Alex, Zach's second and security guy. He didn't think he'd met the female wolf. His trio of teenagers gave submission to Alex, who huffed at them then jerked his head back the way they'd come. Two of them headed out, the third rubbing his nose along the female wolf's muzzle. She nipped at him, but then herded him back toward the house.

Alex turned his attention to Adam, gave a little bow, then turned toward the house. Adam loped up to him, and they ran together after the others. It didn't take long to get to the house where he saw a woman holding a mini-van door open for the wolves to get into.

She waved cheerfully at Alex and him and drove away. Alex led him to a stash of sweats and they changed.

"Thanks, I left my stuff over at Hillary's."

"I figured. You find the boys in any trouble?"

"No, just too tired to turn back to wolf. They were headed back, it was just a slower journey until I helped them change back."

"Ah, that makes sense. Though, why change to human? Testing their strength?"

"Actually, I think they just wanted to go swimming."

"There's a part of the river that's good for swimming, on a day like today there's usually others there. They should have been able to get help to change. They must have gone to a different part of the river for some privacy."

"That's the impression I got."

They'd walked to the house and Alex led them to an office, coded in at the locked door, and closed it behind him. Adam took a seat on the sofa and accepted the bottle of water Alex offered.

"Thanks."

"My guess is they didn't realize that changing back when you're out with the pack, they're getting a boost from everyone changing together, especially the stronger ones."

Adam hadn't known that either, though he couldn't say he'd given it much thought. He also didn't figure this conversation was the reason Alex had led him to the private office. He waited.

"I have a friend out in Los Angeles who's looking at where she can move on. Her power's growing and she doesn't see a place for herself in her pack for much longer. She's fourth, ex-military, and a security specialist, like I am. I use her for the business sometimes when I need someone out that way on the ground and don't want to send someone."

Adam had no clue where this conversation was headed. "Okay."

Alex studied him for a moment. "You're not thinking of going out there?"

He didn't hide his surprise. "Los Angeles?"

"Arizona. Or New Mexico."

"Why would you think that?" A flash of distaste colored his question.

"I didn't mean disrespect," Alex assured him.

Adam waived that away. "No, really, why would you think that?"

"Until the pack is reformed and solidified in some way, the hot topic is going to be who's moving there. It's rare for there to be essentially a whole pack forming from scratch. So people, like my friend Jen, start to get that itch inside, and think that if there isn't a way for them to move up in their home pack, maybe it's time to move on. If there weren't this possibility of a new pack, she'd probably start thinking about traveling more, visiting other packs that she has a connection to, see if there's a place, maybe even a mate, out there waiting for her to find."

"All right, that makes sense. But I don't know what it has to do with me."

"Well, they're going to need an alpha. A strong one. Nothing will really happen until then, and the rest will sort of flow from there."

"I'm not an alpha."

Alex's laugh was genuine, but he bit it off when he saw that Adam was serious. "I want to call you sir, that's how much of an alpha you are."

"I don't mean power," Adam argued. "It takes more than that to lead a pack."

"Yeah, it does." Alex studied him over his water bottle as he took a drink. "Weren't you a teacher?"

"Yes."

"A good one?"

"Yes."

"Hm. All right, well, I appreciate you giving me a few minutes of your time." He stood and opened the door.

Adam just looked at him for a moment, gave a mental shrug, and walked out. He left the borrowed sweats in a pile of dirty clothes by the back door and changed back to wolf. It didn't take long to return to Hillary's house.

He checked his phone, but there were no messages from Myra

about when she might be coming out. Thoughts about seeing her again, being with her again, had him setting the shower to colder than he usually preferred, but he didn't think playing the masturbation game with her again was a good idea. For either of them.

It didn't take long to follow the directions Hillary had left to her shop, and soon he was pulling up to a small warehouse east of Main Street. Hard rock music, the kind he'd never had a particular fondness for, blared through the space, competing with the sound of some sort of electric saw. It looked to him as though they'd finished setting everything up and she'd decided to get some work done. Her hair was pulled into a French braid and she wore protective glasses as she bent low over the noisy machine that was spitting out sawdust at an alarming rate. A man was at an angled table, pencil in one hand, coffee mug in another, as he studied a paper on the desk.

He was pretty sure Hillary knew he'd come in, but she focused on her task. The man looked up as Adam moved farther inside. He blinked a bit, then offered a smile, gaze fixed on Adam's chin.

"Hey," Adam said.

"Hi. You must be Adam. I'm Stephen."

"Nice to meet you."

They looked over at Hillary as her machine turned off and the rock music became the only sound. She picked up a tiny remote and aimed, the sound pulling down to reasonable volume.

"Adam, hey, how was your morning run?"

She pulled her glasses off and wiped her face with a cloth she pulled from her back pocket. Stephen pointed all over his own face, indicating she'd missed a few dozen spots, and she stuck her tongue out at him. She looked at her watch.

"Actually, tell me at lunch, I'm starving."

He waited while they put stuff away, locked up, and then they walked a couple of blocks over to an Italian restaurant. A woman greeted Hillary and Stephen by name and they were quickly seated with waters and menus. Hillary gave him a minute to make a selection, then popped her chin in her hand and repeated the question.

"It was a nice morning. Good run. Nice woods."

She laughed. "Word's already out that you found three miserable boys walking the walk of shame."

"The walk of shame?"

"Naked through the woods because they overestimated their ability to change back," Stephen said.

He frowned. "People will really give them a hard time about that?"

"Nah." Stephen shook his head. "It's just what they're feeling. They might get a little teasing from their friends, but that's it."

"It's not altogether unusual," Hillary added. "Part of growing up. Though, they were deliberately vague when they told Jason's mom that they were going to run out to the river and go swimming. They knew she was going to assume they meant the pack swimming spot, not that they were going to find their own spot."

Adam shook his head. "We only got back half an hour ago, and you already know everything?"

"The joys of pack life," Hillary laughed.

"Sounds great," Adam said with skepticism.

Stephen smiled. "It definitely has its upsides, I promise."

They ordered their food and Adam resumed the conversation. "Alex says there's talk about making a new pack in Arizona."

Hillary frowned but Stephen nodded. "He told me wolves all across the country that are in the hierarchy, or ready to join the hierarchy, will do like a self-evaluation. Take a minute to look at their situation and decide if it's time to consider a move."

"But, nobody from here would leave, would they?"

Stephen laughed. "It's not all about you, Larry, no matter how much Zach tries to let you think otherwise."

She smacked him on the back of the head. Mildly.

"Okay, I guess I can see how people would want to evaluate. But we should be good here. I don't think anyone is coming up to a power level where they might think hierarchy, and the current hierarchy is good."

"Yeah, that's what Alex said. But the way he explained it to me is think about how Molly and Travis are growing in power now that they're mated. They're strong, but you guys are stronger, and growing as well, so it's not an issue. But if you'd topped out, which you will eventually, and they were still growing, getting closer and closer to your power level, you'd all start to evaluate. If this was years in the future and you were older than them, you might consider retiring. If not, they would need to consider where they could go."

Hillary pursed her lips. "Okay, I guess I can see that. They would check to see if there's another alpha out there that is ready to retire, but doesn't have a strong enough first to take over."

"Exactly."

"And the possibility of a new pack has everyone taking a look at their situations," Adam added.

"Right."

"I thought Myra disbanded the pack, though. Why would she do that if there was just going to be another one?"

"I think her first priority was to find healthy and safe homes for all the current wolves, get that situated. But the territory itself still needs to be covered. Neighboring packs can divide it up, but then they have a lot of acreage to keep an eye on," Stee mused.

"Alex said nothing can happen until there's an alpha," Adam said.

"I wonder if Myra has to approve someone. Or the National Council?" Hillary suddenly got a big grin on her face and looked to the door. Zach walked in and headed straight for them, his gaze locked on his wife.

Adam glanced at Stephen, who rolled his eyes as the two kissed hello.

"We were just talking about what's going to happen in Arizona. If they want to form a new pack," Hillary told Zach. "Would Myra have to approve an alpha?"

He stole her water and considered his answer. "Myra, or Marco, if it's after next week. If she approved an alpha, it would be pretty much up to that person to gather a pack, though I imagine because of the situation, she would be more hands-on than normal. It would depend on who it was, really."

Hillary frowned, so Zach continued. "Say you and I decided we were done with Idaho, and we thought Molly and Travis were ready to be alphas. If we went to Myra and said we wanted to be alphas of Mesa, she would probably approve and just ask us to keep her updated on who we accepted into the pack, especially any wolves from the original Mesa pack. She might make some suggestions, or ask us to consider some particular candidates, but that would be about it."

He paused as someone walked past their table, then continued. "But say it was the first of, I don't know, Miami, who approached her. Her name is Taneesha. I've met her, she's pretty strong. But she's not experienced as an alpha, isn't mated, so maybe if Myra thought she would be good as the Mesa alpha, she would approve it, but be more actively involved in the pack's development."

"Okay, I guess that makes sense," Hillary said.

"How much interest do you think there is in starting another pack?" Adam asked.

"I'd say it's unlikely it will go more than six months without one. Or to officially parcel out the territory to neighboring packs. But Myra is probably figuring it makes more sense to let Marco make the initial decision, since he'll need to do the follow-up. So she's not actively searching for anyone. I haven't talked to Marco to see if he thinks it's better to let the momentum build on its own for a bit, or try to direct it from the beginning."

Adam thought about what he'd learned, and what Alex had said, as the food arrived and the others discussed a new business that was moving into town. The surprise on Alex's face when he'd said he wasn't an alpha. And then asking if he'd been a teacher. He'd enjoyed being a teacher, very much. Had worked with high school students and mostly managed to earn their respect as well as that of his fellow teachers.

Still, he'd pulled so far back from that life, after the attack, he hadn't even considered ever being in that kind of situation again. The kind where people looked up to him, relied on him, respected him.

He pushed the thoughts away, shook his head at Hillary when she gave him a questioning look, and returned his attention to the group.

WHEN CINDY OPENED her door to Myra, she did so with a martini in hand. Myra loved her best friend and had to laugh. Cindy always seemed able to read her mood and know if Myra needed iced tea, beer, wine, or something fruity. She'd never made martini's before, but Myra knew instantly it was exactly right.

They managed a good hug without spilling the drink, which Myra accepted and moved into the living room. She kicked off her shoes, curled up on the couch and took a healthy sip. Yeah, just right. She sighed and looked to Cindy who mimicked her on the other end of the couch.

"I don't know where I'm at. I feel like I'm at some sort of crossroads and I don't know why or what to do."

"You do know why."

Damn it. "Adam."

"Definitely Adam," Cindy agreed. "I'm surprised you're having such a strong reaction to someone who's not your mate, but I think you need to acknowledge it for what it is. Just because you're not mates doesn't mean you can't have a fantastic relationship."

"But what if he then finds his mate?"

"Okay, that would suck, big time. But it doesn't seem likely that both of you would be having such strong feelings for each other if he had a mate out there. And besides, are you going to turn away from this on a what-if?"

"Honestly, Cyn, I don't know if I would survive. At least with Eric, I was young, and I knew he'd had no choice, that if he could have stayed with me he would have."

"You didn't have to feel rejected, on top of the loss," Cindy guessed.

"Exactly."

"I get what you're saying, and I certainly understand why it scares you, I just don't think it's very likely. You've known people who've been in relationships when they met their mates. Those original relationships are never really serious. Ever. It's just not how it works."

Myra thought about it. "No, I guess not."

"It's just not the way it works. There's magic involved, you can't forget that. Don't discount it."

"It's not the only concern, though. I don't think he's ready for anything like this. I want him to be. Not just ready for a relationship with me, but ready to join a pack and experience all the amazingness of that, of who and what we are."

"Why don't you think he's ready?"

"Uh, because he basically lives as a hermit? He's stayed away from all wolves, and packs, to the point that Bitterroot didn't even know he was living nearby?"

"That was before. Didn't you say he went to the pack to discuss the problem in the woods?"

"Yeah, but then he ended up solving it himself and not even letting us help. And practically pushing me out the door."

"Mm, hmm," Cindy said significantly, watching Myra over her drink as she took a sip.

"What? Oh. You think that was about running away from *me*, not the pack. Well that's not exactly flattering."

"I beg to differ. He wasn't scared of the pack. He was scared of what was happening between the two of you."

Myra leaned back at that. "Huh."

Cindy raised her eyebrows at her.

"Okay, you might be right."

They drank in silence for a minute before she blurted out, "He called me last night."

"Is that right?"

"I sort of pushed him into agreeing to me coming out there."

"How much pushing was involved."

"Not much."

"Mm, hmm."

Myra laughed. "Maybe he is ready. But he doesn't know it."

"Now *that* I'll agree with. I mean, it took him a while to recover from what happened. Understandable. And the way he dealt with it was to burrow in, protect himself. Also understandable. But it's hard to know when the time comes to pull yourself out of that. I'd say it usually takes some outside influence to make that happen."

She set her drink on the table and hopped off the couch. "Be right back."

Myra took another healthy sip of her martini and considered her decision to go see Adam, rather than give him more time. The question had popped out of her mouth yesterday before she'd had time to censor herself, but she was glad it had. Especially since he'd said yes. But it was time to admit to herself that she had strong feelings for him, stronger than she'd ever experienced for a wolf that wasn't her mate, and that had to mean something. She'd be failing herself, and Adam, if she didn't explore those feelings.

Cindy returned with a carefully balanced plate of fruit, cheese and chocolate. It was beautifully put together, and Myra gave it much appreciation before snatching up a piece of chocolate. Dark-chocolate-covered marzipan, her absolute favorite. It was good having a best friend who was into food.

"Thanks, Cindy."

"You're welcome." Her friend made a couple of cheese-and-cracker combos, then sat back on the couch, popped one into her mouth, and looked at Myra. "I've been thinking about change."

Myra blinked. "Okay. In what way?"

Cindy ate another cracker, looked thoughtful. "It started with the news about Mesa Pack. I was looking on the database to see what information we had about them, you know, just to get an idea?"

Myra nodded. "Sure, I did the same thing."

"There wasn't a lot on there, as I'm sure you saw, so I looked online, at the area."

Myra laughed. "Me, too. I should have asked you to just do the research for me."

Cindy shook her head. "You would have wanted to see it all for yourself, too."

"Good point."

"I guess it was just interesting, looking at the photos of desert and forest, so close together, so unlike here. And I realized I didn't know any of the people listed on the pack roster, not a single one of them. Which wasn't surprising, of course, given what we learned, but it made me think how complacent I've become, growing up here and never moving more than a few miles from my parents' house. Going to school nearby and then coming right back home."

"We've traveled," Myra pointed out, though she understood Cindy's point. "We went to New York, London, Copenhagen."

"Yeah, and that was enough to feel like we were doing interesting things, not stuck in a rut. And we've done a good job of setting up our lives, becoming good at what we do. We're successful women, who've planned for our futures, our retirements, settled into a good pack that works well and loves us."

"So what are we going to do with the next forty-plus years of our lives?"

"Exactly!" Cindy said, putting her drink on the table and clasping her hands together. "I mean, I'm sure we'd be happy and there would be new challenges of some sort that we could come up with, but I was looking at my future and it suddenly seemed so...stale. Maybe part of it is that I haven't found my mate, and that would change things. But I've always refused to live my life in a holding pattern, waiting to see what this supposed guy was going to bring to the table. And I realized I'd sort of settled into that, by accident."

Myra finished off her drink and grabbed some cheese. "Only because you've achieved everything you set out to do."

"Right. So, now I have no more goals?"

There was a reason she and Cindy were best friends, and Myra could feel the tiny tingle of rightness moving through her blood. She scooted closer on the couch.

"I wasn't in Mesa for long, and I was disappointed that I didn't get to explore it more. It's hard to balance being close enough to a city to keep your pack employed and healthy, and yet close enough to the forest to have the room to run and grow, but Mesa seemed to have what it takes. Plus, I mean, how cool would it be to run in the desert and the pine forest on the same day?"

"You really thought about all of that? About what it would be like to live there?"

"Yeah. Not necessarily because it was Arizona. I mean, I have nothing against the state, it was just…somewhere new."

Cindy seemed eager, but wary. "You've been to several new places this year. Have you considered what any of them would be like to live in."

"All those places were great. I enjoyed running in the different pack lands, meeting the different packs. But none of them…" She hesitated, wanting to get the right feeling across without sounding pretentious. "I think, none of them needed me."

Cindy smiled. "Us. None of them needed *us*."

Myra reached out and Cindy was there, hugging her with a squeal of excitement.

The feeling of peace settled into Myra like she'd just been waiting to hear those words. The way she'd felt off, ever since Arizona had happened. She'd blamed some of that disconnect, that uncertainty, on meeting Adam. Before that, she'd blamed it on needing to find him, on not wanting to leave that loose thread hanging before the end of her term. But now she knew the real reason. Her heart had started to shift its loyalties from the St. Louis pack to a new one.

"Thank god for you," she said. "I don't know that I would've even realized what it was I was searching for; and now to find it, and know that we'll be figuring it out together, that's so huge."

"I know, I didn't know if you would think I was crazy but I've been doing all this searching online, for Arizona and New Mexico, and looking at every post in the forum written by any of the pack, and even though I love it here, our pack, our families, I'm ready to try something new. And I remembered that I've been clever enough to succeed at a career that I can do from anywhere I want. I had no clue you'd consider leaving, and walking away from you as my alpha was going to be tough."

"I think that's part of what's been growing inside of me," Myra admitted. "The pack is ready for Kendra and Deacon to take over. They didn't need me at all this year, it's almost as if I've already taken on an advisory role rather than being the true alpha."

"And you haven't heard from anyone thinking about offering up to be alpha out there?"

"No one. And I know the current hierarchies. There really isn't anyone ready to make this kind of move. Except me, because of Kendra and Deacon, and because I've been alpha here for a long time, because I started young, but I'm not ready to retire."

"Do you think Kendra and Deacon were considering it?"

"I'm sure they thought about it, but I don't think they'd want to leave their families here. The kids are still so young and both of their parents are very active with them. But they must have talked about it, because they've been feeling that push to be more, do more. I'm sure of it."

"It's meant to be. This calls for a change-up." Cindy grabbed their empty glasses and marched to the kitchen, Myra at her heals. She put the glasses in the dishwasher and opened the fridge, pulling out a bottle of champagne. Myra got them flutes while Cindy popped the bottle open with expertise. She poured with a flourish and they toasted.

"To new adventures and not being fuddy-duddy old ladies," Cindy said.

"To embarking on our mid-life crises together," Myra added.

They drank and danced around the kitchen like fools for a good five minutes before Cindy grabbed the bottle and led the way back to the couch.

"So. What does this mean for you and Adam?"

Myra frowned. "Well, like you said, I can't hold off on planning my life for what might happen with a guy. And if he was going to fall madly in love with me and move to St. Louis, he can fall madly in love with me and move to Arizona or New Mexico. I mean, even if we'd been mates, I wouldn't have been able to just go lone wolf and live with him in a tiny cabin on someone else's territory." She nibbled her lip. "But, bad shit happened to him in Phoenix, maybe he would hate being in that part of the country."

Cindy nodded her agreement, handing over a cracker and cheese. "Maybe. Maybe not. Will you tell me about him?"

"I think he's convinced himself he's a loner, not a team player. But inside, he's still a high school teacher, I'm sure of it. He was his brother's best friend, and port in the storm. His instincts are to help, to be involved, even when his brain tells him to walk away."

She stretched out on the couch, back against the arm, feet bumping Cindy's thigh. "He's charming, though I doubt he realizes it. Holds doors open for strangers, super polite to waitstaff, doesn't start eating until I do, that kind of thing."

"Okay, he might be good enough for you," Cindy said with a smile.

"He reads. A lot. A lot a lot."

"Better and better."

"I wasn't exactly paying attention because I was kind of out of my mind at the time, but I'm pretty sure I got at least two orgasms for every one of his."

"Now we're talking!" Cindy tipped her glass to Myra, then emptied it in one gulp.

Laughing, Myra continued, "He makes my insides shiver and my lady parts quiver."

"Woo!" Cindy poured them both full glasses. "Tell me more!"

Myra was laughing so hard she was worried she would spill, so she quieted down long enough to take a big drink, then screeched, "Lady parts!"

Cindy collapsed against her and picked up Myra's phone from where she'd tossed it on the table. "Selfie!"

Myra grinned at their image on the screen. "We're blurry, that's not going to look right."

"I think that's you, not the picture."

"Remember when we were young and we thought forty was old and that old people sat around their living rooms drinking tea and discussing politics and gardens?"

Cindy snorted, snapped a couple more pics. "Of course, if we were actually cool, we'd be doing this on Snapchat with dog ears and bunny noses and stuff."

"I don't even know what that means." Myra howled with laughter.

"That's 'cause you're old."

"Not as old as you," she said indignantly.

"Yes, but I work online and I'm hip to these things."

"I don't think you can be hip if you're saying hip."

They dissolved into giggles and finished off the bottle of champagne.

Cindy weaved her way to the kitchen with the empty bottle and Myra picked up the phone. She scrolled through the pictures, squinting to try to make the pictures focus better, selected one that had Cindy holding the bottle of champagne up to her lips, Myra raising her glass to the camera, and texted it to Adam before she could stop herself. See, forty really wasn't that different than twenty.

WAKING up on her best friend's couch wasn't exactly a normal occurrence for Myra, but it wasn't completely unheard of. The good news was she only had a very mild headache, thanks to her fabulous metabolism. She cracked open the bottle of water Cindy had left for her and took a couple of long drinks. She heard the shower turn on and smelled coffee brewing in the automatic coffee maker, and promised herself she could have a cup *after* she finished the water.

She reached over for her phone and pressed the button to see what time it was. The clock showed seven-ten, but her eyes were riveted to the little notification screen that said only two words.

Challenge accepted.

Hastily she swiped the screen to get to the text messages from Adam. The last message had been received at one in the morning, with those two simple words. The only activity previous to that was the picture she'd forgotten she'd texted, until now. It wasn't blurry at all, Cindy had been right. Myra was laughing in a way that mostly only Cindy managed to bring out in her, her eyes sparkling as she held her champagne glass toward the phone. Cindy had tipped the bottle back and was pretending to drink directly from it.

Myra finished her water and struggled to understand Adam's message. She remembered her words. Would never forget standing on his cabin porch, telling Adam that she wanted more for him than existence. She wanted him to actually experience life, to be happy, not just alive. "I challenge you to live," she'd said. And he was accepting her challenge.

In response to her picture? Or was that just a coincidence?

"What?" Cindy asked.

Myra nearly jumped. She'd been so focused, she hadn't heard her friend come into the room. She looked up and her eyes were huge, she could feel it, as she tried to process what he'd meant.

"I don't—I'm not sure. Adam texted me, but I don't know what he means exactly. I think," she swallowed. "I think he means he wants to try. Being together. But I could be wrong."

"Call him."

Myra bit her lip. "Maybe. But maybe it would be better in person."

"Hmm. Could be. Finish your water and take a shower, don't try and make any decisions when your brain isn't awake."

Myra thought the message had shocked her brain as awake as it had ever been, but she did as Cindy suggested anyway, taking the mug of coffee her friend offered her. She tossed the water bottle into the recycle bin and headed to the bathroom. She hadn't come up with a single plan of action by the time she was dressed and back in the kitchen. Her wonderful, amazing, fabulous best friend was just putting two plates on the table, which already held a carafe of orange juice and a platter of melon slices.

Of course, all of it was presented beautifully, and Cindy took a minute to snap some photos before they dug in.

"I probably shouldn't be thinking of this as a done-deal yet, right?"

"Not quite. I need to speak to Deacon and Kendra, see how they feel. Talk to my mom and dad, just because. I think Kyle might not be ready to move from fourth to third, but the pack is plenty strong enough to have that position vacant for a while."

She ate some of the delicious omelet and looked at her friend. "Seriously, you managed a crab-meat omelet in the short time I was in the shower?"

"What can I say, I'm magical."

"Truth. Anyway, I don't foresee any issues, but you never know."

"Also, truth," Cindy agreed. "You going to see your parents today?"

"Yeah. And then I think I'm going to fly to Idaho. I'll only have a day before I head over to California for the ceremony, but I'd rather take that day now than wait until after to go see him."

"Okay, well, keep me up to date and let me know if there's anything I can do on my end."

Myra swallowed another bite of deliciousness. "I think you've done your part, here," she said, forking up more.

It was early enough that she could be reasonably certain her parents hadn't gone anywhere yet, but late enough that they would be up, so she headed straight for their house. On the way, she called one of her pack members who was a travel agent. They worked out the flights and when she pulled up to her parents' house, she texted Adam.

Arriving today 5:25pm; leaving for CA Sun 11:25am.

One night, one full day, and one morning. Hopefully that wasn't asking for too much. Pushing too hard. She turned the phone to silent and went inside.

Her parents were at the table, clearly just finishing breakfast, but her mother offered to make her more.

"No, thanks Mom, I stayed at Cindy's last night, and she made breakfast."

"That's okay then. That girl certainly can cook. It amazes me she prefers to spend her time typing stuff on the internet rather than actually cooking."

"She likes the cooking to be for fun, and not having the pressure of making her living from it."

"I know, I just don't understand these blog things and how she can make money from it."

"That's all right, her accountant understands it well enough," Myra said with a laugh.

Her father folded his newspaper shut and gave her his attention. "What's up, sweetpea?"

"Cindy and I are thinking about making a change. It's...pretty radical." She drew in a breath. "We're actually thinking of moving to Arizona. Or New Mexico. The new pack."

Her father blinked at her and her mother gasped. "Leave St. Louis?"

"That's right. Try something new, change things up a bit."

"Us downsizing the house is a bit. You changing packs is a lot more than a bit."

"But is it a bad idea?" she asked, knowing the answer, but wanting to hear her parents' opinion.

Her mom sighed. "No, it's not a bad idea. And it will mean more travel for us, which is good. Get us off our rumps occasionally."

"Maybe we can get one of those RV things," Dad said. "Drive out that way, see the country."

She listened to them debate the merits of various methods of travel, gave her opinion on how many miles a day it might be reasonable to drive, and what the ideal turn radius might be. Eventually, she gave them both hugs. "I have to head out, I'm flying to Idaho this afternoon and then California Sunday for the transfer. I need to talk to Deacon and Kendra first, see what they think."

"You know they're ready. That's partly why you want to leave, isn't it? Need to leave, because you feel them ready to take over."

She kissed her dad's cheek. "Yes, I've been feeling it for a while but couldn't quite pin it down. Now it all makes sense. But I need to talk to them." And she needed to call Marco in California, make sure he was on board with the plan. It wasn't her intention to saddle him with a decision as she exited the leadership. She wanted his input.

Her conversation with her firsts went exactly how she'd expected. Surprise and even a little upset at the idea of her leaving, then a calm understanding, a knowing that it was right. By the time she left, they were excited, though a little tearful. Well, Kendra and Myra were, at least. She would miss them, greatly, and knew it would be some time before she found such easy cohesion with her new hierarchy, whoever they might be.

She checked her phone, which had beeped while they were talking, pulled up a text from Hillary. A picture appeared, of Alexis and Adam playing cards at a table, a huge grin on Alexis' face, Adam's tipped back as he laughed. Her heart fluttered. She studied Alexis' expression, so happy with how far the girl had come. Then she double-tapped on Adams face, making it big enough to fill the screen.

His laughing face, his pleasure, his happiness, did funny things to her insides. Her nose tingled and she pulled the phone away, took a deep breath. Now was not the time to get emotional. She needed to call Marco and discuss her thoughts on being the alpha for Arizona, it was a call that deserved her full attention and shouldn't be made while packing or driving to the airport.

She went to her office and set her cell phone aside so she wouldn't be tempted to pull up the picture again. Though she hadn't expected any opposition, Marco's enthusiastic support and the sense of relief that the Arizona problem wouldn't actually be a problem, were gratifying. He assured her that he would be around to help in any way possible, but that he couldn't think of anyone more capable to tackle a brand-new pack.

Pleased to be appreciated, she got up to go pack, grabbing the phone. Hillary she could talk to while she was packing.

Her friend answered immediately. "I just heard you're coming out to visit before heading to California, that's so great."

"I'm excited, too. Although, I have to be totally honest and admit that you're not the one I'm most looking forward to spending my time with."

Hillary laughed. "I'm really, really glad things seemed to have progressed with you two. I was about to try introducing Adam to some single women to get his head out of his ass, but you brought it home yourself."

Myra growled.

Hillary laughed again. "He insisted on picking you up at the airport by himself, but I made him promise to have you here in time for dinner. It's supposed to be dinner with the hierarchy, but they won't mind you two being there." She lowered her voice, though Myra was pretty sure she was alone on the other end. "I didn't tell Adam this, but I thought it would be good for him to be at the dinner, just see how the hierarchy gets along, you know?"

Myra thought it wasn't a bad idea at all. "That works for me. And that reminds me, I didn't even ask you if I could stay at your house again."

"Well, you can, of course, but I was thinking you guys might want to drive out to the cabin that Peter owns. It's about an hour and a half from town, but it's not a terrible drive and it will give you guys privacy."

"That's very generous, thank you so much."

"Absolutely."

"And thanks for sending that picture earlier. I just…I don't want you to get too far ahead of yourself. Or of us. I'm not certain he's ready for—"

"No, don't say it. I promise I won't push anyone anywhere they don't want to go. I'm just excited to see two people I like be happier than they were before."

Myra wasn't entirely sure she believed Hillary would manage to not push, but she let it go. "All right, I need to finish packing and head out to the airport. I'll see you for dinner."

She finished quickly, made a couple more phone calls, and headed out the door.

CHAPTER EIGHT

By the time Myra landed, she'd made a list of any wolves she could think of that she might want to approach regarding a move to Arizona. Or maybe they'd start fresh, in New Mexico. She forwarded the list, and the question on which state, to Cindy, for her friend's input.

She helped the woman ahead of her retrieve a carry-on bag from the overhead bin, then made her way off the plane and into the airport. It was a small airport and it wasn't long before she spotted Adam. A spike of insecurity hit her from nowhere. Last time she'd seen him, he'd been pushing her away. Hard. They'd only had a couple of phone calls and a few texts since then. Had she been stupid to open herself back up to him, not to protect her heart more?

She didn't realize she'd come to a full halt, staring at him, until his mouth quirked up and he raised a finger, curled it toward himself in a come-here gesture. Gaze locked with his, she did as he bid, until he reached out and yanked her to him. His mouth was on hers in an instant, her bag dropping to their feet so she could wrap both arms around him and hold on tight.

When someone behind her cleared their throat meaningfully, she pulled her mouth free. "You pushed me away," she blurted out.

"I know. I was scared."

"What does this mean, now?"

"I don't know."

She nodded. She couldn't blame him for not being able to tell her their future. "Let's get out of here."

He picked up her bag before she could and held out a hand for her. Charmed, she accepted, then wrapped her other hand around his arm, snuggling in as they walked. "Sometimes when I'm around you, I feel like a foolish twenty-year-old. It's not necessarily a bad thing."

He looked down at her. "Sometimes when I'm around you, I feel like a foolish fifteen-year-old. It's not usually a good thing."

She laughed and took a bracing breath as they walked out into the cold air. He led them to a car and put her bag in the trunk. "Did you want to drive?" he asked.

"I don't care either way." But she was impressed he'd asked, and he'd managed to sound sincere, like he would've handed her the keys if she'd asked. Wow.

He nodded and opened the passenger door for her, then went around to the driver's side. She waited until they were on the highway before bringing the subject back up. "I don't want you to think I'm expecting any kind of commitment. I just want to see how things might go, you know?"

He reached over and picked up her hand, brought it to his thigh, held on. "I think we're on the same page, Myra. Don't worry so much."

Her nose did that tingling thing again. "It's hard not to. I'm not usually a wuss, but you scare me."

His eyebrows shot up his forehead and he looked at her. "Don't you have that backwards?"

She smiled wryly. "I guess it's fair if we scare each other."

"You're the one who's supposed to have her shit figured out. I'm the fool who's been living outside of life for a long time. I might need some help finding one again."

"You know I'm happy to help with that, but I don't want you to feel pushed—" She broke off. "Well, that's not true, I did push, because sometimes people need that, but I meant that for you, and life in general, not where I'm concerned."

"I know. I needed to get hauled out of my rut. Thank you for that."

She wiggled her nose to keep the tears from forming. "Now that you've left your cabin for a little vacation, will you tell me what you're thinking about your future?" She made a concerted effort to not hold her breath while waiting for an answer, and wondered if she shouldn't have waited until they were stationary to bring this up.

"I've been thinking about things, while I'm out here. When you left the cabin, the idea of going to St. Louis, visiting you there, meeting your family and your pack. I'm not going to lie, even though it makes me a coward, the idea seemed ridiculous. No way I could handle that."

And now? she thought, but pressed her lips so he could speak at his own pace.

"I came here to Idaho out of a sense of duty." He glanced over at her. "You knew that. Used that."

"Hell, yes."

He smiled and turned back to face forward. "And you knew I would find more than that. Understand what I could be a part of. If I wanted it."

"Yeah." She said it softly, felt the tears come as his hand squeezed hers.

"I'm not saying I want to audition for packs to join and start taking care of others when I'm not sure I'm great at taking care of myself. And I'm not saying I'm going to pack a bag tomorrow for St. Louis. But I'm saying I would like to come visit you. Assuming you don't get your fill of me here and decide you've had enough."

She sniffled, impressed she'd held it back for this long.

"Hey," he said, putting on the turn signal and checking over his shoulder to ease them to the side of the road. "What's this?"

"I'm just happy for you. And for me. But mostly for you."

He used his thumbs to wipe the tears from her eyes.

She dug through her purse, found a tissue. "I would love for you to come and visit me. But, I'm wondering if you would mind visiting me in Arizona, instead of St. Louis. Or maybe New Mexico."

"I don't really care where I visit you. Are you going to help get a new pack settled? Alex mentioned there was talk of that happening. Actually, he asked me if I was going to be the alpha."

"Oh. Oh!" She turned more fully to him, pulling her leg up onto the seat. "That's an amazing idea. I was going to do it, but if you're interested, I can stay in St. Louis."

"I wasn't really interested."

"Are you sure?"

"You really think it's a good idea for a guy who hasn't worked his way up through the hierarchy to suddenly be alpha to a whole pack?"

"Hillary didn't work her way up, and she's just as much alpha as Zach is."

"Yeah, but she has him there to help her."

Myra shrugged. "If you had a good hierarchy, which I would help make sure you did, you would be fine. I'd have no doubts about your ability to handle it."

He was quiet for a minute, and then he cleared his throat. "I'm not really interested, but it means a lot you'd say that." Checking over his shoulder again, he moved back into the highway. "Why are you thinking of leaving St. Louis?"

"I guess I've been in a bit of a rut, myself. I was pretty young when I become alpha, I've been doing it for a long time. I love my pack and my family, but my life has essentially been the same for the last ten years, and there's no reason to think it's going to change anytime soon. At most, some of the hierarchy might move away, but it wouldn't really change much for me."

She took a deep breath. "What happened in Montana, it sort of woke me up to how stale things have become."

He sighed. "Did I tell you I was sorry about that?"

"No, don't be. I really enjoyed our time. I'm not going to say it didn't hurt, the way you ended it, but I totally understand. That was a lot for you, in a really short amount of time. I think you handled it pretty well, all things considered."

He threw her a skeptical look and she laughed. "No, really. You got poisoned, were seriously ill, met me, which, you know, is huge." She laughed when he rolled his eyes at her this time. "And hearing about Arizona and Hillary and Alexis, and all while feeling enormously attracted to me, I'm sure it was very overwhelming."

"Okay, yeah, we'll go with that," he said, dryly. "By the way, we're expected at dinner tonight, with Hillary and Zach and some of the others. Not exactly how I was planning the evening to go, but I was overruled."

She smiled. "I heard. I also heard they offered us a place to stay that wasn't a houseful of other sharp-eared werewolves."

"Reward for agreeing to sit through the dinner."

"Ah, you'll have fun. You enjoy their company, admit it."

"We'll see how I answer that once I have you alone."

"Uh huh." She reached to the radio and fiddled through Hillary's preset stations, until she'd tried them all. Then she tried the search button and didn't stop until she hit the Eagles, and finally sat back. She pretended not to notice his shoulders visibly relax at her selection, turning her laugh into a small cough.

"You haven't told me what you do," he said as they turn off the highway.

"Oh. I record audiobooks."

"Well, you don't hear that every day. How did you get into it?"

"A friend of a friend needed someone to do a cheap voiceover spot, so I helped out. I enjoyed it, and decided to look into the whole thing for some side money. I wanted to buy a house. I was doing office work for a shoe company owned by one of the pack elders at the time. Eventually the side money was good enough for me to buy the house, and then quit the office job and focus on it full time. I settled into audiobooks, mostly fiction."

"That's great that you get to do something you enjoy."

"Absolutely. I mean, it's definitely work, and sometimes it feels like it, for sure, but I love the flexibility. I can schedule projects to what works best for me, do the recordings when I want as long as I meet deadlines I've helped set, and I don't have anyone hanging over me all the time." She glanced over at him. "Will you tell me more about this whole stealing-from-drug-dealers thing?"

"I was being a bit of an ass. I don't really do that anymore. I did do it a couple of times, early on when I needed money and when I had absolutely no doubts where the money I took came from. I also made huge donations in the drug dealers' names to various charities."

"Why doesn't that surprise me?"

He looked over at her but didn't respond. He drove up to the Jenners' gate and punched in a code. Before long Hillary was admitting them into the warm house, low music on in the background, delicious smells coming through from the kitchen and the low hum of several people talking.

AFTER GIVING MYRA A HUG, Hillary grabbed Adam's arm, leaning in close while she walked him back to the large kitchen. Travis was pulling two pans of what looked like chicken out of the oven. Molly was using tongs to stir around a large pan of green beans on top of the stove, Zach was pulling bottles of beer out of the fridge and already had a bottle of wine tucked under his arm. Tracy, Alex and Stephen sat at the island, munching on something Adam couldn't identify. He could see Aaron and Peter in the dining room, setting the table. Hillary moved to help Zach and Myra took a seat at the island, so Adam followed suit.

Myra scooped something up with a bit of bread and offered it to him. He eyed the bland looking substance skeptically.

"It's hummus," she urged.

Shrugging his shoulders, he accepted the bread and popped it in his mouth, pleasantly surprised to enjoy it. It didn't taste at all like the baby food it resembled. He vaguely listened to Myra and Stephen discussing favorite hummus brands and considered what a hell of a turn his life had taken in the last week.

Here he was surrounded by powerful wolves, one stronger, two equal, and several just beneath him in power level, and he wasn't in the least worried about it. He didn't have any concerns about losing control of himself, or of those around him losing theirs. On the one hand, everything seemed very normal, very traditional and familial. On the other hand, there was no doubt that they were werewolves and the room held a great concentration of power and strength. But none of it set his radar active.

Well, Myra did. But not because she was stronger than him. His awareness of her was sexual. But more than that, he had to acknowledge as she slid the hummus closer to him, handed him a piece of the bread, all without interrupting her conversation with Stephen. Even though part of him wanted desperately to be alone with her, to be tearing her clothes off just enough that he could thrust into her, slam her back against the wall, knowing she could take it, wanted it, pounding into her—Well, shit. He shifted uncomfortably and tried to redirect his thoughts. Because while they were a very real idea of what he wanted to be doing, he'd also enjoyed talking to her on the drive down, didn't mind sharing this little island with her and being offered food by her while listening to her and Stephen discuss the relative merits of a food processor.

He felt Alex's gaze on him, met the other man's eyes. Found a twinkling amusement and understanding. Zach came by and plopped a bottle of beer in front of him, one hand resting easily on Adam's shoulder.

"Drive up and back was okay?" he asked.

"Fine." He leaned to the side a bit so Zach could get to the food. "It's a nice drive."

Zach nodded around his bite. "We like it out here. Perfect blend of out of the city but close enough to get to the airport, or for some of the pack to commute. Close enough to have some big clients for the security guys." He pointed his chin at Alex.

"We keep an apartment in the city," Alex said. "And rotate personnel through every week so that there's always someone available to get to the client right away, if they have a system issue. And backup only an hour out."

"Makes sense."

"The hardest part for packs that want rural like this, I think, is the jobs and the schools," Myra said.

"Definitely," Alex agreed. "We're big enough that we can sort of take over the school district, if we need to. I think in my parents' day they practically ran the school board, because they weren't happy with how things had been going. Even now we have a couple of pack members in district management, one who's a principle at the elementary school most of the pack goes to."

"Size helps, for sure," Zach added. "Although smaller packs can blend more, don't need as many jobs, they still need nearly as much land to run on."

"I suppose that's why you don't get too many groups trying to break off and make their own packs?" Adam asked.

"Right. It's theoretically possible. They would petition the council, and it would depend on the current pack that holds the territory they're looking at, but it doesn't happen often and those are some of the reasons why."

"Any word on what's to happen in Arizona?" Alex asked just as Travis called out that it was time to head to the table.

They grabbed their drinks, settled in at the table and quickly filled their plates before Myra answered him.

"Actually, there has been a development about Arizona," she said, letting the others in on the conversation they'd been having. "I've decided to leave St. Louis and take it on. I'd certainly be interested in any opinions you all have about those who've expressed interest in joining the new pack."

"Wow, really?" Hillary asked.

Adam was surprised by the doubt in her voice but Myra only smiled.

"You're wondering how I could leave my pack?" she asked her friend.

"Yeah, I mean, I know I haven't been doing this long, but the idea of walking away from my people is kind of shocking. I don't mean —" She broke off, frowned.

"I understand completely. It never occurred to me I would be ready to step away before it was time to retire, but these things have their own cycles. I've been the alpha there since I was twenty-eight. We've grown and changed together, and Kendra and Deacon, my firsts, have really grown since they mated a couple of years ago. Normally they would start looking at other packs who were going to need a new alpha, who didn't have a strong enough first to take over, but this time, it feels right to do it this way. I'll miss them, of course. Miss my family and friends. But part of being the alpha is knowing, bone deep, what is right for your pack, and this is it."

"Wow," Hillary repeated. "I get what you're saying, it just feels weird. But I'm excited for the new pack. Will you bring back any of the Mesa members?"

"There are definitely a few that I'll check in with. I'll talk to the alphas I've placed them with, see how they've been doing. Especially those that had jobs they loved out there, and had to abandon, extended families, that sort of thing."

Stephen frowned. "So they get a pass on letting what happened, happen?"

Hillary reached out and rubbed his arm with a smile. "Breaking the pack up wasn't about punishment. Their new alphas were responsible for appropriate punishments. With Myra's oversight."

"Exactly. Breaking the pack up was about making sure everyone was under a capable and appropriate alpha, and because there was no one who could just step in and deal with the entire pack as it was. I would never have asked anyone to do that, and even now, saying I'll take on a pack in Arizona, or New Mexico, while I will be willing to take in some of the old pack, there will be wolves from all across the country who are interested in a change and will ask to join. Each will be evaluated on their own."

Adam understood what Myra was saying in theory, but he wasn't sure how he felt about her having any of those who'd essentially condoned what had happened to him as part of her pack. But, he was willing to give her the benefit of the doubt that she knew what she was doing.

The conversation turned to those that the hierarchy had heard about who might want to join a new pack, including Alex's friend from Los Angeles. Myra excused herself to grab a notebook and pen, and noted down the info and advice she was given about each wolf mentioned.

Adam ate while he listened to Alex tell Myra about his friend Jen, as well as a conversation between Tracy and Peter about one of their teenage wolves who was having some school trouble, and how they could help him. He had to admit, it was a side to pack life he'd never imagined or considered. It put what Myra was wanting to do in a whole new light. Hell, it put what she was already doing in that same light. He hadn't much thought about what it meant for her, or Hillary, to be pack alphas. His only thoughts on the matter before had been that alphas were the people in charge, calling the shots, and should be blamed if anything bad happened in the pack.

When he'd sent her the text encouraging her to come visit, he hadn't really thought about her actual day-to-day life. Hadn't really thought about much beyond seeing her again, to be honest. He'd just needed to see her again.

As if she understood the directions of his thoughts, she flashed him a smile that somehow managed to convey sweetness, amusement and heat. Or maybe he was projecting. Hell if it mattered, he just knew he wanted to get her alone again. And not while driving.

Molly, sitting next to him, gave him a little shoulder bump. "We haven't managed to overwhelm you. I'm impressed."

"Was that your intent?" he asked, deadpan.

She looked nervous for a whole second, then decided he was messing with her. Obviously she was used to having brothers. "I was worried, though, for real. We knew you weren't in the habit of living with a pack, but Hillary said you'd be fine." She blushed. "Not that we were talking a lot about you."

He gave her a return shoulder bump. "I know. I like that you guys worry about other people's feelings and needs. It's what you do. It's admirable."

She gave him a relieved smile. "You're pretty good at it yourself."

"Let's get dessert," Hillary said, springing up and grabbing her empty plate as well as Zach's and Peter's. Half the table followed suit, the other half deciding—like him, he assumed—that too many people in the kitchen would just be annoying.

He looked at his watch. Determined they wouldn't be staying long once dessert was brought out, even if he was enjoying himself. He caught the smirk on Zach's face, which actually reminded him that he needed to thank Peter for the use of his cabin. When the other man came out with several portions of the pie, Adam made eye contact.

"I wanted to thank you for letting us use your cabin. Hillary loaned me the key."

"Hey man, happy to. I love that it gets used, since I don't get out that way as often as I'd like. Especially while I'm single."

Adam wasn't a huge fan of apple pie, but this was served with good ice cream so he was relatively satisfied. But he ate fast. He glanced up at Myra and found she was on pace with him and telling Hillary thanks but no thanks on the offer of coffee. Oh yeah, she was with him all the way. When he finished, he set his fork down with more of a clatter than he'd intended. Myra didn't look at him but she smiled.

Hillary did look at him, laughter in her eyes. "You guys should head out soon, it's a bit of a drive."

He rolled his eyes, but didn't contradict her.

WHEN THEY FINALLY MADE IT to the car, he had to laugh. He hadn't been in a situation like that since he'd been in college. Of course, he hadn't exactly had a group of friends since he'd become the wolf. Suddenly, he missed his brother. He wasn't sure how he would have handled the situation if his brother had still been alive, but it would've been interesting.

A soft wave of compassion washed over him as Myra reached over and put her hand on his arm. It should probably bother him that she could send stuff at him. But it was nice.

"Why are you sad?" she asked.

"I was just thinking about my brother. What he would have been like with that lot."

"A good thought?"

"Yeah."

"Do you believe in an afterlife?"

"I did. Even though my parents were religious assholes, I did believe in God and heaven."

"But."

"But I didn't believe in werewolves. So, then I wondered if I maybe had it backwards. Now I'm leaning more toward neutral. And I remind myself that people should be good regardless of what they claim to believe in. It's their actions that matter."

"Well said."

"How come you're staying on your side over there?" he asked.

She laughed. "I don't trust myself to be closer. I might get ideas."

"Oh yeah? What kind of ideas?"

"The kind that could make us crash and die."

"We're kind of hard to kill," he reminded her.

She chuckled. "Well, I might be willing to risk it, but I find I'm not much willing to risk you."

A fist squeezed his heart tightly, but he reached over and pulled her hand into his.

"I was thinking earlier that a lot has changed for me in the last week, but I guess you're in a similar boat. Ending your term, making the big move, starting a whole new pack. That's all pretty big. Making time with a dirty old werewolf."

"It is. But it's all good things, even though some of it will be a lot of hard work."

He didn't make the easy joke. "I know you'll put your heart and soul into doing it right."

"Yes," she agreed. "All of it."

"You said your friend is planning on going with you?"

"Yes, Cindy. She's my bestie, as they say these days. She's amazing, and it was talking to her that really sealed the deal for me on what had only been a vague thought before. And she'd been thinking the same thing, so it really worked perfectly."

"Is she hierarchy?"

"No, a regular pack member."

"Just her? No mate?"

"That's one of the reasons she wants to get out of her comfort zone, explore more of the world. She hasn't met her mate yet."

"How long have you known her?" he asked.

"Oh, wow, about ten years I guess. We became friends pretty quickly. It's hard to imagine her not in my life, but I think both of us still would have made this change without the other. Especially in this day and age, with being able to see each other when we phone, and texting, all that."

"Hm, that reminds me. Any of those books you've narrated have sex scenes?"

She laughed. And laughed. And didn't answer the question.

As they got closer and closer to their destination, he found himself, strangely enough, relaxing more and more. At the start of the drive, he'd have figured he'd be ready to throw the car in park and have his way with her. Instead, he was planning all the things he might do to her. Starting with the hood of the car. No, that would be too hot after the long drive. Maybe there would be a porch rail he could bend her over. No, he didn't know the area, hadn't scouted it. Too dangerous to be distracted outside. He'd get her inside, secure the door, and then he'd start.

Things didn't go exactly as planned because at the last minute, when he closed the car door, he remembered they had bags. He tossed the key that Hillary had given him to Myra and grabbed their bags from the back. By the time he reached the door, she'd opened it, stepped inside and turned on the light. Perfect, he was able to see as he set their bags by the door, made sure it was locked, then turned to her.

Her look was open invitation and wanton heat. Oh yeah, she was ready for him, and he was back on plan. He stepped to her, smiling when she reached for him, but not stopping until he had her pressed against a wall. She scrabbled at his shirt, but he just cupped her face in his hands and brought his lips to hers. She stilled, everything but her lips, which opened for him. He caressed her cheekbones with his thumbs while tasting her, exploring her.

She sighed, her body melting into him. He moved one hand to the nape of her neck, used that thumb to tease the edge of her jaw, pressed his leg between hers. She whimpered and got her hands moving again, trying to work his shirt up without his cooperation. He nipped her lip, nibbled his way to her ear, sucked in the lobe. She gasped, her hands stilling on his waist for just a moment, before resuming with renewed vigor.

He pushed his thigh into her, letting her rub her clit against him. She managed to get his shirt up to his armpits, so he relented and pulled back enough for her to push it over his head. He flexed his thigh and she dropped her head against the wall with a moan. He really liked her sounds. He wanted more of them. More of her. He pulled her into another kiss, but slipped one hand down her back to tease the waistband of her skirt.

She was moving on him now, grinding against his leg, her hands gripping his sides tightly. He slid his hand down her cheek and grazed her neck lightly. She shivered against him, then gasped when he made it down to her breast. He palmed her through her shirt, letting his hand warm her until she was moaning with need. Then he gave a squeeze, at the same time pressing his thigh more firmly into her. She ripped her mouth from his and came with a short cry.

Music to his ears.

Adam unbuttoned her blouse and pushed it off her, pulled her into his arms and walked her toward the stairs while she was still recovering. His dick felt like an iron rod, but he was determined to have a bit more fun with her before he really let loose.

He eyed the stairs. Carpet. Excellent.

"How you feeling, baby?" he asked.

She blinked up at him, gave him a slow, happy grin, palmed his pecs.

He chuckled, slid one hand into her hair, gave a light tug. Her eyes went to half-mast and her nails dug in deep. He used his hand in her hair to turn her to the stairs. "Up you go, two steps."

She tried to turn her head to look at him, but he didn't let her. He kind of wished he could see her face, but he had plans. When she'd gone up two steps, he stopped her, leaned in close to her ear, and whispered, "Now get on your knees."

Her sharp intake of breath and the smell of fresh cream from her body made up for missing the expression on her face. She placed her knees on the step, careful to pull her skirt free first, then leaned forward when he urged her to. He let go when she'd rested her arms along another step and turned to look back at him. The lust in her eyes was surely mirrored in his own, but he didn't look for long, instead focusing his attention on the sweet ass displayed for him.

His palms ran over the cotton of her skirt, shaped the perfect globes. Perfect for *him*. He massaged until she began to wiggle then he bent forward and bit her through the cloth.

"Fuck me, please," she begged.

"Mmm."

He put his hands on her ankles and ran them up her legs, drawing her skirt up to her waist. He laid it over the small of her back and enjoyed the site of the lacy green underpants. Then he ripped them off.

"Oh my god!"

"Just me, baby."

She barked out a laugh, looked at him again over her shoulder.

"*Please* fuck me now." She widened her knees farther along the step to make sure he fully understood the idea.

He smiled at her, slid a finger into her slick channel. Drew it out and tasted it.

Her mouth dropped open and her eyes went wide. "Adam," she begged, a whisper this time. But he heard her.

He pulled his finger from his mouth and teased her clit with it. She rested her head against her hands and moaned. His thumb slid into her, teasing her opening while his finger worked her clit. When her legs started shaking, he eased back, trying not to smile at her little wail.

He opened his jeans and pulled his cock free, enjoying the way her eyes glittered at him as he fisted himself, guided the head to her wetness, teased her some more. She growled, pushed back as much as she could though it wasn't much. His thighs held her steady, but he'd teased her enough. He pushed into her, seated himself in one thrust.

"Oh, fuck, yes!"

"Stay still, Myra, I don't want you getting rug burn on your knees."

She growled again.

"It's okay, baby, I'll do the work."

He gripped her hips and began to move, rocking slowly at first to make sure she was ready, then harder when she pushed back for more. The slapping sounds of flesh meeting flesh didn't drown out her nearly constant moans and pleas for more. He gave her more until she cried out, her channel spasming around him in release, then gave himself to the sweetness of her hold. He dropped down over her, elbow braced next to her head so he didn't smash her into the stairs.

CHAPTER NINE

Myra needed to get off her knees. Carpet was better than wood, she was sure, but it wasn't good for long. She pushed up on her hands, ran into Adams chest. He wrapped an arm around her and stood, supporting her until she could get to her feet and make her slightly numb legs work well enough to climb the stairs. She would never look at stairs the same way again, that was for sure.

They staggered to the top and Adam nudged her to the left. She assumed Hillary had given him specific directions because he guided her to the second door, and inside. It was probably a lovely room, but mostly she just noticed the queen-sized bed and headed straight for it. The slate-blue comforter with sunny-yellow accent pillows was charming, but she'd barely processed it when Adam's hands were turning her, lifting her onto the bed. She scooted back against the pillows and welcomed him into her arms.

He kissed her again, as he had earlier, with no sense of urgency. That had worked out pretty well for her, so she went with it, sliding her hands into his hair, rubbing her heels up his legs. Wait, he was still wearing his jeans. She pulled her mouth free and shivered at the wanting expression he gave her.

"Take your pants off," she suggested.

He frowned, glanced down at himself then rolled off her, off the bed. She stripped off her skirt and bra, while he shucked his shoes and jeans. She quickly pulled the bedding down, stacked the pillows and arranged herself against them. She opened her arms, wanting more of the kisses, but he wrapped his long fingers around each of her ankles instead. Kissed one knee, then the other. Slid his hands up to tickle lightly at the back of her knee.

She nearly kicked him in the nose, and he quickly changed tactics, rubbing his slightly stubbled chin along her inner thigh. The feeling was almost unbearable, but so was knowing where he was headed. He slid his hands along the outside of her legs and underneath to cup her butt. Then he lowered his head to her clit, pulled it between his lips. She ground her heels into the bed, fisted the sheet in her hands.

God, he was too much. She could feel him, feel the connection she had to him gaining ground inside her, taking hold in a way she wouldn't have thought possible for someone who wasn't her mate. Hell, if she hadn't already been mated once, she would be convinced he was hers. But, though the feeling, the connection, was tremendous, it was nowhere near the level of the real thing. She couldn't complain, though. It was amazing, feeling even this much of him inside her.

He nipped her sensitive flesh and she lost all thoughts beyond what he was doing to her. His tongue speared into her and she brought her hands to his head, holding him still as he worked his way inside her. He moaned into her flesh and she gasped. His fingers tightened on her butt, lifting her even closer to him as he devoured her. She slipped a hand free of his hair, brought it to her clit and rubbed. Her knees closed against his head as the sparkling feeling shot from her clit, to her core, then spread through her whole body. She arched and screamed, slammed both of her hands back to the bed to hold on tight as he continued to work her.

"Okay," she panted. "No more."

He gentled, placed soft kisses to her lips, her clit. His fingers relaxed and slid free from underneath her. He kissed his way up her belly, between her breasts, and finally reached her mouth. A long, slow kiss while she caught her breath, her legs boneless, her brain fried. Finally he kissed the tip of her nose and flopped to her side, pulling one of the pillows under his head.

She blinked at him.

"Um."

He grinned, reached down and pulled the sheet and comforter up. He pushed one arm under his pillow and rested his head on it, watching her. Then he snaked his other hand under the blanket to rest on her breast. She managed to huff out a laugh.

"This is a nice place."

"Is it?" she asked, cheekily.

"From what I could see. I'm not picky, anyway, so I'm sure it's nice enough for me."

She raised her eyebrows. "Do I strike you as high maintenance?"

"Nope."

"Hmph."

Her eyes drooped, and she let them close for a minute, let her mind drift. It was nice, being with him. New but comfortable. Simple but engaging. She didn't want to waste it sleeping, so she roused herself, opened her eyes to find him watching her still.

"What's your favorite movie?"

"*Billy Jack*."

That woke her up. "Really?"

"Sure, why not?"

"Because it was released before you were born?"

"Before you were born, too."

"And?"

"I liked it. I'll admit, I haven't seen it in years. But hey, I was a teacher who wanted to help kids, living in an area that experienced its share of racism."

"All right, fair enough."

"What about you?"

"Favorite movie? Hmm. *Goonies*."

He grinned. "Good one."

She reached out and traced his smiling lips with her fingertip. "Where's the farthest you've ever traveled?" she asked.

"Canada. My parents took us to Nova Scotia when we were in high school."

"Sounds cold."

"We went during spring break. It was a nice change from what we were used to in Phoenix."

"You stayed close to home. I'm surprised, after Jamey died."

"It was a big enough place that I didn't feel like it mattered that they were there. I had no trouble avoiding them, since we definitely did not frequent the same places. I wanted to be in the school district that I'd grown up next to. Felt as if I could do some good there."

"I bet you were an amazing teacher."

He didn't *quite* blush, but his eyelashes swept down to his cheeks. "I like to think so."

She traced her finger over his jaw. "I can't believe how much more centered you feel, than the last time we were in bed together. It wasn't just from you being sick, was it?"

"No. I've changed. I don't fear myself anymore. I hadn't, for a while, I guess, but I hadn't stopped to realize it, either. And I don't fear what others can do to me, anymore. It's…freeing. Thank you, for that."

"I don't think it was me, really."

"You helped."

She smiled, ran her hand along his neck, scratching lightly. "Good."

"No siblings for you?" he asked.

"No, just my parents. Some aunts, uncles and cousins out on the East Coast."

She traced his shoulder, circling the muscles of his upper arm.

"Would you ever be a teacher again?" She ran her palm down his pecs to his nipple, circled it with the tip of her finger.

"I don't think so. I don't think I'd trust myself."

Frowning, she met his eyes.

"Not because of the students," he clarified. "The administration and some of the parents. I'm not sure I could compromise enough to make that work anymore."

"Ah. If you wanted, you could get involved with the pack kids. Teach a class, or coach basketball or something. There's always a need for more adults to take a roll."

He didn't say anything and she tugged her gaze from his pebbled nipple back up to his eyes, worried by what she'd find.

Warmth. Acceptance. Happiness.

"It means a lot that you would offer that."

Surprised, she leaned in and kissed him. "Whatever role you might choose to take, I have full confidence you would do some good in people's lives. But I don't say that to pressure you into taking any role, if you don't want to."

"It's probably too late for me to just go back to my cabin and pretend no one outside of it exists except to offer obstacles on my trips to the store."

"Probably." She smiled as she pulled his nipple between her thumb and finger, gave it a little twist.

"And online friends are nice and all, but turns out actually talking to people is kind of nice, too."

"Mm, hmm. And touching people," she added, teasing her fingers through the hair on his chest.

"That's nicer with some more than others, but yeah. I'd read about it, the whole werewolf touch thing, but I didn't really believe it."

She started to nod, then frowned. "Read about it?"

He blew out a breath. "Oops."

"You'd already been on the website."

"Well, yeah. Are you mad?"

"Nope." She explored the contours of his abs, tickled lightly along his side, as he'd done to her leg earlier. Every muscle in his stomach tightened delightfully. She explored his hipbone, prodding at it with her thumb, then smoothing it with her fingertips. She had to scoot down a little bit to reach farther and encircled his half-hard penis with her fingers, her grip as light as she could make it. He grunted, reached down and closed his hand over hers.

She hid her smile in the sheets, watched, enthralled, as his larger hand covered hers, slid her hand up and down his length. Feeling him harden beneath her, his hand guiding hers, was amazing. She fixed the pillow under her head better, so she could watch without straining her neck.

His breathing picked up, and so did hers, as they both watched their stroking hands. She pressed her thighs together to try to relieve the renewed need there. He gave her hand a squeeze, then pulled his away. She kept sliding hers up and down, but he used his to urge her chin up for a kiss. Happy to oblige, she lost herself in the rhythm of stroking him and being kissed by him, the hardness versus the softness. He was fully erect now and she caught a bead of pre-cum from the tip, smoothed it down over the shaft.

He growled and she knew she had no more time to indulge, gave him a good squeeze before he pulled free, rolled on top of her, urging her higher up onto the pillows. His mouth came back to her and she pulled his lip between her teeth, gave a little nip. He responded by tweaking her nipple until she gasped, freeing his lip. His fingers slid into her, two of them twisting within, testing her readiness. She bucked up to meet them, ready for more.

Pulling free of her grasping hands, he kneeled up between her legs, grabbed her ankles and brought them out to her sides, bending her nearly in half. She was spread wide open and they both watched as his cock met her entrance, slowly disappeared inside. He pushed her legs back more and she cried out as he rubbed against her insides in all the best ways. She clenched her muscles tight when he began to pull out, and he groaned. Then, it was all she could do to hang on, to take what he gave her. She put her hands above her head, braced against the wall as he pounded in, gave her everything he had, took her hard and fast and completely. She cried out, her neck arching back as she tried to process the delicious release, so much, too much, so right. So very right.

He released her legs, came down to her as the orgasm powered through him. She held his head in her hands, kissed him with everything she felt, everything she needed to give him. Gave him her love. She felt their connection, a fraction of what it would be with a mate, but a gift she treasured nonetheless. She stilled a moment, hoping he wouldn't get scared, wouldn't pull back.

His kiss intensified, and she relaxed, giggling with joy as she wrapped her arms around her man.

THEY SLEPT TANGLED TOGETHER, then took a hot shower that woke her up in all the right ways.

"I need food," she groaned, pulling on her clothes when he'd retrieved their bags from downstairs. "Lots and lots of food. How far do you think it is from somewhere with food?"

He smiled at her. "Hillary promised it's only ten minutes away."

"Whew."

A short trip to the local diner got them breakfast, followed by a grocery run to get them through the rest of their stay. They didn't have much time together and she preferred to spend it at the cabin, not at restaurants where they had to watch what they talked about. And be fully clothed.

When they'd put the groceries away, she suggested a run in the woods. "Actually, this reminds me. I gave the info about your bad guys to one of my people to monitor. They haven't reported back with any issues, so I assume everything is good. Have you been keeping track, too?" she asked as they surveyed the woods from the cabin's porch. Nothing concerned her, so she began to undress.

"Yes. One of them tried a new email address, thinking I couldn't monitor him that way, but I quickly disabused him of the idea. Other than that, they've kept out of trouble."

He pulled her into his arms when they were naked, kissed her hard.

"Are you worried," she asked softly, not sure what he was thinking about.

"About the hunters?"

"No, about this. Being in the woods with me. Being wolf together."

He rubbed her back, his hand warm against the cool morning air. "No. I want to see your wolf, run with her."

She smiled, stepped back, and let the wolf be fully present. He watched her, waited until she was furry to run his hands over her again. Not cold anymore, she luxuriated in the feel of his hands rubbing through her fur, scratching behind her ears. Not something she would let most get away with. She yipped at him, and he changed. His larger body bumped against hers, encouraging her down the steps. She nipped his neck, then took off, the exhilaration of running through the forest never old, but the joy of doing it with him by her side a new level of perfect.

They explored the area, laughing in the way of wolves when they flushed out some wild turkeys, chasing a rabbit with no intentions of catching it, eventually circling back to the cabin, where they took a nap on the edge of the woods, in a large sunny patch, curled together in their fur.

She woke to the sound of his stomach growling and was laughing as she turned back to human, watching as he did the same. He shoved his face in her belly, growling and nipping. "No laughing at me, I'm a badass alpha, haven't you heard?"

"A badass alpha who needs to eat. Grate the cheese for me, and you can do that sooner, rather than later."

"Deal."

She chopped the onion first, got that cooking and added the meat while he grated cheese. There wasn't a huge spice collection in the cabinet, but she made due, leaving behind the cumin she'd bought at the store for the next visitors. While the meat was cooking, she chopped up some cilantro and gave Adam the lettuce to deal with.

"Just so you know, if I was doing this at home, there wouldn't be these jars of salsa and guacamole, I would have made those from scratch."

"Good to know. Just so *you* know, I do cook. Not so much in that cabin, I admit, but my previous place was on the grid, and had a real kitchen."

"What's your specialty?"

He pondered that for a minute. "Fried chicken. It's the only thing my mother taught me that I embraced. It was her mother's recipe."

"We'll have to try that sometime." She stirred the meat then handed him the salsa and guacamole to open and put on the table, tossing the package of tortillas over. "At home I also would have gotten corn tortillas and fried them, but we're going for soft flour this time."

"I can work with that."

She smiled at him as she drained the meat and put it in a bowl and motioned him to the table. He'd already set out sodas for them, so they were good to go.

You could learn something about a man from how he put his taco together, she mused, watching him overfill the tortilla so that he really had a burrito that barely closed. She spread the guacamole on her tortilla, then the meat, lettuce, cilantro and salsa. Damn, she'd forgotten sour cream. Ah well.

They ate in silence for a few minutes, then built their second round. She glanced over at him while he worked, debated if now was the time and place, but couldn't get it out of her mind. She *knew* she couldn't be the only one feeling this way, but... "So. I don't want to push or anything, but I would like an idea of how you see this going forward."

He frowned. "You shouldn't feel as if you can't push me. It makes it sound like it's on me what we do next."

"Fair enough. I think I'm falling in love with you."

His hands stilled in the act of rolling his tortilla closed and he looked at her. It was hard to read his expression, but she didn't sense panic or anger or anything negative, so she waited.

"Think?"

She narrowed her eyes at him. "Well, it's not the norm for werewolves. Once you mate, you sort of leap into love, so it's not like it was for me before. But I can't imagine going through my days without knowing you're going to be some part of them, so I'm wondering how you think that might go."

He abandoned his plate and reached for her hand, twining his fingers with hers. "I don't want to hurt you," he started, making her stomach clench. "I don't know that I'm ready to abandon my home and move to St. Louis with you. And I'm really not sure how I feel about returning to Arizona. But I do know that I want to keep seeing you. I can't imagine going back to a life that you're not a significant part of."

Relief moved through her almost like an orgasm. She smiled and squeezed his hand. "That's good enough for me."

"But it's not what you want."

"Hey, if you suddenly declared that you were giving up everything and moving in with me, I'd wonder if you were sick again," she teased. "I don't have expectations on how we move forward, I'm just really glad to know you're with me on wanting to move forward at all."

"I'd be pretty happy just staying here for a while, but I know that you have responsibilities. Being alpha isn't just a title for you."

"No, it's not. It comes with responsibilities. And joys."

He grunted his understanding from around a big bite of his burrito. "It looks good on you," he said when he'd swallowed. "I can't think of anyone I trust more to see to building a new pack out there." He cocked his head. "I suppose that's not exactly a ringing endorsement when I only know a few alphas. But still."

She smiled. "But still. Thanks."

He took a drink of his soda, eyed her. "I think I've never felt like this with anyone. I think I can see myself leaving my little cabin to come visit you. Often."

"That makes me happy."

"Good." He nodded, as if it was settled.

And she supposed it was. He'd come a long way in a short time, and she wasn't going to ask him for more. Didn't need more, for now. Knowing that he would come visit her, would welcome her visits to him, was pretty huge. Although, she wasn't sure how long she'd be able to wait. It was his fault he was so damn good at sex. And cuddling. And napping in the sun. And entertaining her through a meal. His own damn fault.

She smiled to herself and reached to make another taco.

After lunch, she attacked him. Pushed him against the refrigerator and rode him down to the floor. Rode him to completion. They lay on the floor, spent, panting, his jeans dangling from one leg, her underwear sitting on the trashcan lid, his top pushed up to his shoulders, hers pulled down beneath her breasts.

They took another shower, managing to do so without sex, and she pulled him back downstairs into the library she'd spotted. Having seen all the books decorating his cabin, she figured she was safe in assuming he shared her love of reading. She wandered back and forth between the three bookcases, picked four novels, and joined him on the couch, where he'd stretched out.

He looked ridiculously sexy wearing only jeans and an old sweatshirt. Bare feet should not make a man look so good, but she apparently had a weakness. Still, they needed a rest, so she stretched out in front of him and offered the books.

"Pick one."

She'd chosen a thriller, young adult fantasy, a lawyer mystery and a cozy mystery. She was going to have to discuss Peter's library with him; she was fascinated by the single man's variety.

Adam read the descriptions of each one, then held out the cozy mystery. She shouldn't be surprised they were so in sync. Though she would have been happy with any of the choices, this one seemed best for whiling away a lazy afternoon. Plus, she was fairly certain there wouldn't be sex in this one, and considering they were managing enough of that on their own, she figured it would be for the best.

She cleared her throat and began to read out loud. She attempted different voices for different characters, which had them both laughing. When she finished the first chapter, she handed the book to him. Snuggling into his chest, she listened as he continued the story. And she fell deeper into love.

How the hell could she resist this man? There was no sense in trying. She would just have to figure out a way to make it work.

Taking her turn on the next chapter, she pretended not to notice when his hand found its way to her breast and settled there. Or when his other hand began to trace a long pattern up and down her thigh. Her voice caught as he eased his hand to the inside of her thigh, closer to her center. And closer. She kept reading, wishing she'd worn her skirt instead of jeans.

He traced the seam and she thought maybe she was reading the same paragraph for the second time. Or maybe not. Who knew? She tried to spread her legs to give him better access, but there was no room. His lips found her earlobe, and she closed her eyes, her mouth open on whatever she'd been trying to say.

"Don't stop," he murmured. "I really like the sound of your voice."

She forced her eyes open and started back at the top of the page, since she had no clue where she'd been. He maneuvered so that she was flat on her back, one leg hanging over the side of the couch, his body pressed against the back, and her. One of his hands was between her nape and the pillow, holding her gently. The other opened her jeans, slid inside her panties.

"Not fair," she whispered.

"It's your chapter," he disagreed. His nose played along her hairline, his breath warm against her cheek. "Read," he reminded her.

She picked a random spot, wondering how long it had been since she'd actually turned the page. She was never going to get to the end of the chapter at this rate. After a couple sentences that she couldn't begin to recount, she remembered that she hadn't actually agreed to follow any rules. She tossed the book to the floor, rolled off the couch and stood, facing him.

He was trying not to laugh.

"Jerk," she pouted.

He opened his eyes wide in mock innocence. She backed up until her butt hit the desk, then eased her jeans off, kicked them at him. He caught them in one hand and tossed them onto the book as he watched her pull off her sweatshirt.

"Take your pants off," she suggested as she eased herself up onto the desk. Spread her legs wide in invitation. He watched her as he followed her suggestion. When he was naked, he began to stroke himself, his gaze never leaving her. She swallowed the saliva pooling in her mouth as he got harder and bigger. He stepped forward, between her legs, one hand going to her hair, doing that little grip that made her weak. His other hand hooked behind her knee, pulling her leg up to rest on his ass.

She tilted her pelvis and he slid inside. His tongue traced along her neck. She brought her other leg up to cross her ankles behind him and braced herself with her hands on the desk. He smiled into her throat—her only warning before he bit the curve of her shoulder.

The shock of it, the bite that mates gave, without the mating, sent a shockwave of sorrow through her. She wanted him to be her mate, mourned that they didn't have that ultimate connection.

He stilled, buried deep inside. She opened her eyes to meet his concerned gaze. Only then did she realize that a couple of tears had escaped. She shook her head.

"It's okay. I'm okay."

His hand on her nape squeezed as he searched her face for more answers. She pulled him into her with her legs, arched her back so her breasts pushed into his chest. He must have felt the truth of her statement, because he resumed his efforts, sliding into her slowly, then back out, kissing her neck, face, mouth, never staying in one place long.

"Please, Adam."

"You please *me*."

Her arms trembled and her legs squeezed, but she had no leverage to hurry things along. "I need you."

"I'm right here," he said on a long slide in.

"Oh god."

"Still just me."

She laughed. "You bastard."

"You're so fickle."

"I swear, no one would believe me if I told them what a comedian you are during sex."

He smiled into her neck again and she tensed, but instead of biting her he picked up his pace. Hard and fast, her hands slipping on the desk behind her as he powered in and out, his body pushing against her clit until she came with a long cry. He pushed through her orgasm, prolonging it, a couple more thrusts until he, too, found completion. He collapsed against her, one hand braced next to hers, his breath harsh in her ear.

They ate the leftovers and she found herself sad as she washed the dishes that they only had a breakfast left to eat together. His hand drifting over her butt as he passed by on his way to the fridge made her smile and push away the thoughts of being apart. When she was with him, she determined, she needed to be with him.

She called Cindy, using the computer. When he wandered into the room, she called him over and introduced the two. He put his hands on her shoulders and leaned in close so that he could see the monitor, gave her friend a smile. Then he patted the desk approvingly and Myra almost had a mini orgasm. When he'd gone out of the room again, Cindy waved her hand as if it was suddenly very hot in St. Louis.

When she'd packed the laptop away she found him on the living room couch, his own laptop perched on his stomach, his legs stretched out. He closed the lid and set the computer aside, holding out a hand for her. She lay down on top of him, her hands on his chest, her chin resting on her hands. His hands immediately came up to her back. She closed her eyes and took a deep breath, simply enjoying the feeling of being held safe and secure.

"I like being with you," he said.

She melted. "I like being with you, too."

"How did the call go?"

"Great. I'm going to make an announcement after the transition, so that wolves interested in joining know to contact me. Cindy's going to meet me in California for the transfer, then we'll head out to meet some of the wolves, especially if they want to be hierarchy, so I have another, trusted opinion. I thought, depending on where they are, you might like to join us on some of the trips. I'll let you know where and when so you can decide."

"That could work. I admit I'm curious about meeting more wolves now. It's not at all like I thought it would be, being here with Mountain Pack."

"I'll be curious to get your opinions on the ones you meet, too. Not just the ones interested in joining, but a fresh pair of eyes on the packs in general."

"Then it's a plan. Let me know when you go to LA, I haven't been there since I took Jamey for his first college spring break."

She scooted up to kiss him. "It's a plan. Want to watch a movie?"

ADAM DROPPED Myra off at the airport and tried to tell himself that he felt normal. It was too early to feel lonely, especially considering he was on his way back to a house full of people. He couldn't have changed so much in such a short amount of time that the idea of going home to his cabin was starting to feel strange. He dismissed the idea that he wasn't becoming a new person so much as going back to the person he'd been before the attack. He was a werewolf now, for fuck's sake. He could never be that innocent human man again.

He turned the radio up, enjoying the station that Myra had selected. He appreciated that they were compatible outside of sex. Most of the hookups he'd had in the last ten years hadn't been so complementary. His fault entirely; he hadn't been interested in forming real relationships, so hadn't made any effort to make that connection with the women he was with. It wasn't the first time he realized what a dick he'd been, but the idea made him more uncomfortable now than it had before.

But hell, it wasn't as if he'd been interested in forming a real relationship with Myra, either. It had just happened.

He made it back to Mountain View in good time and accepted an invitation from a few of the young adults to go for a run. It wasn't until he was on his way with them that he understood he'd been placed as the adult in charge. One of the mothers had asked if he'd mind going, since she had an errand she needed to run...and now here he was. Trusted by the pack to look after teenagers, and trusted by the kids to see to their safety. Both were somewhat daunting, now that he realized it.

He shook off the idea. They were on pack land and both groups knew that. His presence was merely a formality. Still. He pushed his human brain away and enjoyed the run, slowing down when some of the kids lingered, speeding up to give one a good race, then circling back to check on the group.

When the smallest started to slow, he encouraged them to stop in a nice, shady spot and they rested for a while before heading back. The return trip was lazier and he gave some playful attention to those he hadn't spent time with on the first leg. When they neared the house, the oldest let out a little howl and someone opened the door to let them in. The kids rubbed past him, their offering of thanks, he guessed, and went to the living room to rest with their friend's watching television. He went back to his clothes, changed to human and dressed.

When he accepted an offer to stay for dinner, he texted Hillary to let her know. She responded that she and Zach would come too, so he moved to join the kids watching a movie in the living room. Jason, one of the boys he'd run into in the woods previously, pulled him aside.

"Hey, I heard you were a comp science teacher. I'm working on a school project, and I'm stuck. Any chance you could take a look real quick?"

"Sure."

They moved to a room that had several kids studying and found a corner where they could talk quietly without disturbing the others. It didn't take long to see that Jason had a good grasp of what he was doing and just needed to be shown a couple of tweaks to be fully on the right path.

"Looks like you have a pretty good teacher," he commented.

"Yeah, we like her. I could have talked to her about this on Monday, but I wanted to get more done."

"Glad to help."

"Hey, so, I heard you're dating the National President."

He raised his eyebrow at the boy, who flushed.

"I just, you know, some of my friends, especially the girls, were saying how there's no point in dating someone who's not your mate. And I, you know, think that's bullshit. I mean, I like this girl at school and if we like hanging out together, why not? Right?"

"Right."

Jason blinked at him, then grinned. "Right. Cool. Thanks, man."

Most of the kids had left for their own homes by the time Hillary and Zach arrived, but he noted how they both spent some time with those that were still around, before moving on to the adults. The pack house was where a lot of the single wolves lived before setting up their own houses, so they were mostly young adults, though he spoke to a couple of random older wolves. He questioned one who told him she'd had her own house for years, but had received a good offer to sell it, so she was staying at the pack house until she found something she felt like moving into.

It was a bit of wolf society he found interesting and he talked to Hillary about it as they shared a beer before dinner.

"It's great, right? The pack contributes some money, especially for food, since everyone is welcome to come and eat. We pay someone a salary to be in charge, make sure there's always someone to cook, that sort of thing. And everyone in the pack always knows they can come here and someone will be around to talk, or run with, or eat with. Sometimes you just want to sit on the couch and watch TV but have someone else be in the room with you."

He nodded and she cocked her head at him. "You aren't nearly as hermity as you were made out to be," she pointed out.

"Yeah, well. I was. I just don't seem to be anymore."

"I'm glad. We all need people."

"Don't you ever want private time, though?"

"Sure. Zach and I haven't been together long, but I know that if I asked, say, Molly and Travis, since they're firsts, to cover us for a weekend or whatever, they totally would. That's why the hierarchy is so important. The whole pack knows they have several people to go to if they need something, it doesn't all just fall on our shoulders."

"Have I mentioned how glad I am that you're happy?" he asked, slinging an arm around her shoulders as they followed the call in for dinner. There were enough of them, but not too many, that they were all eating at the massive table he'd been told she'd built for Zach as a birthday present. He took a seat next to her and started filling his plate.

"You have. And I must say that you seem better than when you first got here."

"How did I seem when I first got here?"

"Tense. Unsure. Prepared to be angry."

He couldn't exactly find fault with that, so he just shrugged as they began to eat. She laughed and jostled his shoulder with hers and turned her attention to her own plate. Aaron and Tracy showed up with Alexis, who squirmed her way onto the seat between Hillary and him.

CHAPTER TEN

Adam and Zach decided to go play pool while Hillary worked. There was a decent crowd for a Sunday evening and Adam was teasing Zach about planning his honeymoon. He was teamed up with Claire, a friend of Hillary's he'd talked to about Alexis, and Zach was with Jonas, a bartender who was there to get in a game or two before his shift started.

"Come on, you can tell us. Europe? Or somewhere tropical?"

"Yeah, I can tell you, and Hillary will find out in, what? Twenty minutes? Fifteen? I don't trust a single one of you to be on my side instead of hers."

Claire laughed. "You always were a smart guy."

Jonas missed a somewhat difficult shot and handed his stick to Zach. Adam lined up his shot and nailed it, but the bounce back on the cue ball was terrible and he had pretty much no hope for his next move. Luckily, it didn't leave much for Zach, either, who scratched. Claire gave Adam a high-five.

"But can we trust him to do right by our girl, that's the question," he said. "He doesn't have any experience being a mate and—" He stopped mid-sentence, frozen in a flood of sensation. Warmth and heat both, need and desire, happiness and joy, fear and sadness, all at once. He knew it as Myra, but that was all he knew.

"You better stop teasing him," Claire laughed. "Hillary's going to punch you."

He smirked but said nothing. He had no understanding of what was happening, and just as soon as he felt it, it was gone. He blinked, clapped for Claire who sank the five ball, and tried to process. Claire made another good shot and turned to him for approval. He managed a "Nice!" and a smile. She looked at him strangely for a minute, but returned her attention to the table.

He grimaced when she missed the next one, and tried to shake off the feeling. He took a drink of his soda, needing something cold, feeling hot and antsy all of a sudden. Jonas made some comment that the others laughed at, but Adam ignored him. It was his turn again and he quickly evaluated his options, lined up his shot and slammed the stick home. The cue ball jumped the table and landed on the floor at someone's feet. Adam growled, then clenched his jaw in an effort to keep from saying something nasty.

The waitress chose that moment to walk behind him, making some comment, running her hand soothingly along his shoulders. He turned sharply, disgusted by the touch, jaw aching with how hard he was working to keep it together.

Zach walked up to him and it took considerable effort not to start a power play with the strong alpha.

"Maybe we should go outside," Zach suggested.

Not liking being told what to do, but unable to deny that something was wrong and he had no idea what the fuck it was, Adam tossed his stick onto the table, enjoying the sound of balls being knocked out of position, and strode out.

He reached the SUV, circled his shoulders, cracked his neck. "Something's wrong," he admitted. He felt hot and angry and… almost out of control. Almost.

"Any idea what happened?" Zach asked.

"I felt…something. It hit me, inside. Now I'm all…frustrated. Fucked up." He scrubbed his hands over his face.

Zach considered him and Adam had the distinct impression the other man was holding back.

"Tell me," he growled out.

Nodding, Zach leaned back against the truck, appearing nonthreatening. As-if.

"A few minutes ago, I felt the transfer of power between Myra and Marco. Just before I took my last shot. That's why I waited a couple of beats, make sure nothing would distract my aim."

"And?"

"And...seems like too much to be a coincidence that you felt something right after that happened. Has to be related."

Adam really didn't want to have this kind of conversation, but he didn't have much choice. "I want to see her. Myra. Now. And I don't like hearing you say her name."

"I see. And that just started?"

Adam ground his teeth together. "She's only been gone half a day. I talked to her this morning. Okay, fine, I missed her. But this." He shook his head. "This is fucked up."

"Well. The good news is we can probably identify the problem. The bad news is that you might not like it."

"Just tell me what the fuck happened."

"All right. I'm guessing Myra is your mate. And when she stopped being National President, it triggered for both of you."

It didn't seem possible that his brain could be crying out *fuck, yes* and *fuck, no* at the same time, but there it was. "Mates are supposed to know each other. And be bonded, once they have sex. We've had sex."

"Yeah. Well, maybe I'm wrong, but it seems to me that the fact Myra was serving as president might have mucked that up a bit. She wasn't exactly, entirely, herself when you met. It's sort of like if you meet your mate when you're in high school, you wouldn't know it. You might feel a strong attraction, love even, but you wouldn't feel the actual mate connection until meeting up as adults." He shrugged. "I'm not saying that's exactly what's happened, but it seems to fit."

"You don't act like this when Hillary isn't around. Hell, she's not around right now." He wanted to punch the truck, see it dent.

"Yeah, here's the thing. I can't think of a time when a mate bond triggered in alphas as strong as you guys, but the two weren't together to consummate it. Every natural instinct and drive in you right now is to mate with her, but she's hundreds of miles away. That's very unusual."

"Why the fuck are so many things unusual and rare but seem to happen to me?"

"Just lucky, I guess. But think about this—you have a mate. That's great news. And you already liked Myra. A lot, I'm guessing. You won't be in the position of trying to get to know someone while also needing to fu— Hm, okay, we won't go there right now."

Hearing Zach talking about Myra and fucking was not sitting well with him. Which was ridiculous. Part of him knew that the other man had zero interest in Myra. The bigger part of him didn't give a rat's ass.

"She was sad." He bit the words out, unable to get past that fact, even though he knew she was a lot of other feelings, as well.

Zach frowned.

"She had a mate, before. Years ago. Died."

"I didn't know that. But it has nothing to do with you and now. Don't hold it against her."

He growled. That wasn't what he'd meant. Fuck, this was getting ridiculous. "I need to…call her, find her. Something."

"I'm surprised she hasn't tried to call *you*."

His brain clearly wasn't working, because now that Zach mentioned it, he was surprised as well. He reached for his phone, but his pocket was empty. Cupping his hands to the car window, he spotted the damn thing in the cup holder, where he'd put it on their drive into town. He growled.

"Easy now," Zach said, laughter in his voice that Adam chose to ignore, since he heard the sound of the locks releasing. He opened the door and lunged for the phone, both worried and relieved to see that he had two missed calls. He tapped on the screen and the phone started ringing.

"Adam! Are you okay?"

He growled. "You?"

"Uh. Yeah. I'm fine. Sort of. I, um, didn't expect that."

He could feel...something, tugging at him. An almost physical link to her that wanted to connect. He tried to rein it in, wasn't at all sure what he was doing. That didn't even account for the itchy heat that was filling him up, the need to move, to be with her, to jump in a lake, *something*. Fuck.

"Adam?"

"You don't sound okay," he said through clenched teeth.

"Because I'm worried about you. And it's uncomfortable, not being with you. I don't know if it's easier for *you*, or worse. I'm sorry. I wish I was there."

"I need to go run," he bit out, working to not crush the phone in his hand. Talking to her wasn't helping when he could hear the fear and frustration in her voice. For the first time since recovering from the poison, he felt as if his control was not completely his. Barely his at all. He fought the fear with logic, but only half won. "I'll call you later."

A pulse of sadness reached him, not through the phone, but it quickly disappeared.

"You should go to her," Zach urged.

Adam clenched his fist. "Won't that make it harder to resist?"

The other man blinked at him. "Well, yeah, I guess if you're not planning on mating with her, it *would* be harder to resist in person."

"Then I need to decide, before I go to her."

"Yeah, Adam," he said softly. "You need to decide first."

"I can make my way back to the house," he said, stepping away from the alpha. He turned and walked into the woods.

Myra and Cindy had been warmly welcomed in Elk Creek. There had been a lovely dinner when they arrived, most of the pack gathering for the ceremony. As was tradition, once the transfer was made, Marco would go for a run with his wolves. He had said some words to his pack, then turned to her. She met his eyes, nodded and held out her right hand. He took it, and she brought him in close, putting her left hand on his shoulder. He did the same, closing their little formation. Gaze still fastened to his, she focused on that little spark of magic, that connection to the alpha wolves across the country, offered it to him. His eyes widened as he felt and accepted the bond. She clearly felt his awe, respect and gratitude for the honor he was receiving, and she had to blink back a tear.

Embracing him fully, she whispered, "You've got this," in his ear and stepped back.

And nearly staggered. Her ears went fuzzy and she was only barely conscious of the wolves howling together, singing out their joy in the moment. She could only feel the terrifying wash of need, the hunger, both emotional and sexual, for her mate.

With the next beat of her heart, she shut it down, hard. She saw Cindy swing around to look at her. Fighting to keep her connections closed off, she waved Marco and his pack off. He gave her a look of concern, knowing she'd meant to run with them.

"I'm sorry, I need to handle something. We'll be all right. Please, be with your pack."

He gave a small bow, then turned to head into the forest. Cindy grabbed her hand and pulled her into the house.

"Oh shit, what am I going to do? What have I done?"

"I don't know, what have you done?"

"He's going to be furious! I can't believe this is happening."

"Can you please tell me what we're talking about?"

"Adam. We're mates."

She jolted as Cindy screeched, "What?"

"Oh my god, oh my god, oh my god."

Cindy put her hands on her shoulders, gave a little shake. "But, you were with him. And you were *with* him. You would have known if you were mates!"

"I think the extra power of the presidency was keeping that from happening. I wasn't fully myself this last year, I was holding the power, or at least the potential of the power, of all the alphas. And I even had to use it, to pull on it, right when I met him. We weren't equals, not then."

Cindy took a deep breath, dropped her hands. "Okay, calm down now. Nothing is going to be solved by hysterics."

She glared at her friend. So maybe that last part had come out a bit high pitched and fast and...okay, yeah, she was nearly hysterical. She forced in a deep breath, pulled her head out of her hands.

"Right," Cindy said. "Finding a second mate is damn rare, but Eric has been gone a very long time, and if anyone deserves it, it's you."

She offered her friend a weak smile. "I can't really process that part right now. I don't—Eric was—" She shook her head. "No, the crisis right now is that Adam is going to hate it."

Cindy dashed to the dining room table, grabbed a pile of napkins that were still out from dinner, handed one to Myra. Who hadn't realized she'd started crying.

"Of course he isn't. That's not how mating works, and you know it."

"I know, but you don't understand. He hates being out of control. Just the amazing day of sex we had the first time made him feel out of control enough to run away."

Frowning, Cindy considered that.

"This is bad, Cindy. I don't know what to do. Do I call him and apologize?"

"You are absolutely not going to apologize for the gift of being mated." She rubbed her hand up and down Myra's back. "Honey. Remember that he's going to be feeling the good stuff, too. He's going to want to be your mate, just like you do." She paused. "You do want to be his mate, right? You liked him?"

"I'm in love with him. I was going to talk to you about that, after we finished here. But Adam. Being pushed into something that he doesn't want is going to be horrible for him. Talk about a loss of control, the mating is like the ultimate loss of control!"

"Well, yeah, but it's an amazing and glorious one. Or so I hear."

She put a hand to her chest, trying to relieve the squeezing pressure in her heart. "I know that and you know that. But it would be a betrayal to force it on him."

Cindy scoffed. "He'll be thrilled, once it's all done."

Myra just shook her head. Though it was nothing like when she'd lost Eric, she actually felt a sense of grief, in addition to the want, need, and desire pulsing through her. Adam was her mate, which meant the last thing she wanted to do was hurt him.

"Okay," Cindy said. "I haven't met him, so let's assume for a minute that you're right, not overblowing this due to the sudden, enormous flood of emotions that just hit you. Do you think that he knows what happened?"

Myra tried to think. "I don't know. I shut down my connection pretty fast, so he shouldn't be getting any feedback from me, but I'm sure he'll be feeling the same need to mate that I am. He just might not know what it is. It's not as if he's human, and only feeling a tiny echo of it. He's an alpha wolf, he'll be feeling it strongly."

"You need to call him, then. Hopefully he's not running around as a wolf and can answer the phone."

Should she try and connect to him through their bond? No, that would just freak him out, if he felt it. She was going to have to actually ask him how he was doing, and then figure out how he *really* was doing, based on his answers. Ugh, men.

She made the call, got no answer. "Okay. We wait."

"Twenty minutes," Cindy decreed.

"Fine."

She dropped her head in her hands again. Her emotions were warring between elation and fear. And she was so worried about Adam that she almost felt sick. She looked at Cindy. "Let's get out of here, I don't want to be here when they get back."

Taking charge, Cindy wrote a note for the pack. They had

planned to stay the night, but luckily they had rented a car at the airport and weren't stuck waiting for a ride. They grabbed their bags and Cindy shoved her into the passenger seat.

"Where do we go? Motel? Airport? Idaho?"

Myra rubbed her forehead. "Let's head to the airport. Hopefully I'll talk to him before we get there and have a better idea of what I need to do."

"Perfect."

She waited a whole minute. "I can't stand it, I'm calling again."

Cindy frowned, but didn't object. They both heard it ring and ring. She hung up when voice mail kicked in, dropping her head back against the seat.

"Shit. God. Shit."

They drove for a few minutes with her watching the clock to keep from calling him again, too soon.

The phone rang, and she nearly fumbled it before answering. It felt so good to hear his voice, but then so heartbreaking to hear how unsettled he was. Afraid. Adam wasn't supposed to be afraid of anything, damn it. And she had caused it. Sort of.

Her stomach turned and she worked harder than she thought possible to hold her feelings back, to not let them travel down the link that already existed. She couldn't make things worse by letting him feel her upset. She didn't think she succeeded entirely, but she could only do what she could do.

He hung up and she clenched every muscle in her body to keep it all in. Cindy's hand came to her neck. "Honey, you have to breathe."

She rocked, trying to do as Cindy said, but also trying to keep the promise to herself not to overwhelm him. Shoving her fist into her teeth, she let only the tears slide down her cheeks, nothing else came loose. She hoped.

When the car stopped, she looked up. They were at a hotel. She didn't object.

"Wait here a minute, I'll go get a room."

She nodded.

It didn't seem as if much time had passed at all before Cindy was opening her door and pulling her out. She walked like a zombie to the room and simply sank to the floor.

"Myra, honey, come over to the bed. Lie down."

She just shook her head and hugged her knees. She would pull herself together. She would. She had to. Just...not right now.

ADAM RAN. And ran. And every mile, his instincts urged him to run the other way. Toward Myra. Somehow, he knew what direction to go to get to her, but the more he wanted to, the harder he resisted, running fast in the other direction.

Part of him knew he was making a mistake. This wasn't a loss of control like he feared. Wasn't the same thing. Maybe. It was the maybe that killed him. He refused to be forced into action that wasn't his choice. Falling for someone was one thing. The sudden compulsion to join himself with Myra, while enticing beyond belief, was terrifying in the way it completely bypassed his brain and maybe even his will. Brought back the horrible fear of being a monster with no control.

He shook his head, knowing that wasn't quite right. The wolf promised it wasn't right. He had never become that monster. But he didn't trust it. Never had. Maybe he'd started to on this trip. But it wasn't enough to counter the years of refusing to do so.

Finally, he compromised, not going to where Myra was, but letting himself make his way to Zach and Hillary's house, even though it was uncomfortably close to the same path.

When he was several miles out, the two wolves materialized onto the path in front of him. He should have sensed them well before he could see them, but he was too busy ignoring his instincts. He'd slowed down, his feet a bit raw from the reckless running. The white wolf came to him, licked his jaw, then turned and led the way back to the house. She went inside and came back a few minutes later with two pairs of sweats.

He didn't need to look at Zach to know he was concerned as

they walked into the house. He dropped onto their couch and leaned back, fingers rubbing his tired eyes.

"Feeling any better?" Zach asked.

"No. Just tired."

"I wish I could help," Hillary said as she walked back into the room.

He smelled chocolate and opened his eyes to see her holding a mug. He blinked. Seriously? Hot chocolate? What the hell.

He accepted the hot drink, sitting upright and cradling it in his hands. He hadn't even realized he was cold. He still felt antsy, but was tired enough not to be as affected as earlier.

"Are you going to keep running?" Hillary asked, her voice free from judgement.

"Can I?"

"I think so," Zach answered for her. "I think if you never saw each other again, it would fade. It would take a while, though. Because of the strength, and I think because you're not strangers. You do have feelings for her."

Yeah, he had feelings for her. It was harder now, to untangle them from the shit pulsing through him. But he had to admit, at least to himself, that before this afternoon, he'd been falling in love. Maybe had even fallen. He'd just been determined not to rush it, to let it take its course. He snorted.

"I hurt her. When we talked on the phone."

"She understands," Hillary assured him.

"Doesn't make it okay."

"No," Zach agreed. "But I bet she's feeling the same guilt. For hurting you."

"She didn't do anything. It's not her fault."

"Won't stop her from being upset that *you're* upset." Hillary gave a small chuckle. "It can be a stupid cycle."

"Yeah, I bet." He sighed, took a careful drink of the hot chocolate.

"Can you tell me what you're afraid of?" Hillary asked gently.

He wanted to. Sort of. But he couldn't get the words out.

Zach got up and put a hand on his shoulder. Squeezed. "I'll be in the other room if you need me."

Hillary came to the couch, took the mug back from him and set it on the table, then curled up next to him, wrapping her arms around him. He fell into her, accepting the comfort and support gratefully.

"I'm afraid to lose control," he admitted finally.

"I'm not going to lie. I can see how it would feel like a loss of control. And maybe in some ways it is. For a second. For the leap of faith. But then, have you considered that together, you'll actually have more control? Be stronger?"

No, he hadn't considered that. He supposed it was true. Myra had already convinced him that there wasn't anyone out there who could force him to do something he was unwilling to. But it sure as hell wouldn't hurt to be more powerful. Unless of course he lost control, and then there would be no one to pull him back. He sighed, knowing that fear was groundless. He wasn't suddenly going to become a monster. He'd already proved that to himself. Absent being poisoned, of course. And even then, Myra had been sure he wouldn't have attacked her if she'd heeded his warnings.

"Are you really willing to walk away from her?"

"She was mated before, you know."

"No, I didn't know that."

"It would be worse, don't you think? Worse than losing someone to death, to have them choose not to be with you?"

"I don't know. I think she would rather know you were alive and healthy in this world, and choosing not to be with her, than to know you were dead."

He grunted. "Maybe."

"It doesn't matter though, does it? Because you love her."

Fuck. He did. He no longer knew if he had that morning, but did it matter when he did now?

"She's hurting, and I can fix it."

Hillary didn't say anything. She pulled free enough to get his drink and hand it to him. He snorted out a weak laugh and took a sip.

"I need to get to her."

"I already looked at the flights. By the time you get to our airport, wait for the next flight, get from the other airport to Elk Creek, you could have driven there. I'll drive."

"She's not in Elk Creek. I think she went to the airport. Or nearby."

"Well, still probably faster. Maybe closer to the same, but you won't be sitting on an airplane trying not to jump out of your skin, surrounded by dozens of strangers."

"Good enough. You don't need to come. Stay here with your mate."

"You're exhausted. Let me drive you while you get some rest. Then I'll bow out and catch a ride home."

"I'm not abandoning you on the side of the road." He looked at her incredulously.

"I think we can work out a better plan than that," she chided him.

"Oh. Yeah. I guess so." He really was tired.

Hillary handed him his phone. He stared at it for a second. Zach must have had it. He hesitated. Once decided, there was no going back.

He shook his head. The lead spikes in his gut, the iron bands around his heart, told him he was already past the point of no return. Now he just needed his woman.

He typed in two words and sent the text.

MYRA LAY ON THE BED, Cindy propped up on the pillows next to her, her thigh acting as a pillow, her fingers sifting through Myra's hair soothingly. When her phone beeped, she snatched it up.

Challenge accepted.

"Oh god!" she gasped, trying not to cry again. She was a badass alpha, she shouldn't be crying this much.

Fuck it, she was a woman who was being torn to shreds, she could cry as much as she wanted. Her phone beeped again. Another message. She wiped her eyes and blinked them clear.

"Okay, he's driving. Hillary told him that would be easier than flying since neither of us has the good sense to be near a major airport right now."

"Take a shower. Then we'll start driving, too."

"I shouldn't make him wait, we need to get going!"

"Don't be ridiculous. He's hours away. It will take five minutes and make you feel a hundred times better. Trust me. I'll work out the route while you're in there."

She gave her best friend a hug. "I love you, thank god you're here."

Fifteen minutes later, they were on the road. Her sense of loss lessened, and she knew that though they were hours apart, they were headed toward each other.

"Will you be upset if he doesn't want to move to Arizona, and we have to change our plans?" she asked Cindy.

"No, of course not," Cindy replied. "I mean, I think it would be awesome if we all start this pack together, but if you can't do it, if he can't do it, another alpha will come forward eventually. It will work out the way it's meant to."

"He might be fine with it," Myra said. "I don't think he was especially tied to Montana, it's just where he was settled at the time."

"Yeah, but Arizona isn't just anywhere for him."

"True."

"See if you can take a nap, then you can spell me after a while," Cindy suggested.

She really didn't think she'd be able to fall asleep, but the next thing she knew it was dawn and she could feel him coming closer.

They stopped for a bathroom break and picked up some food to eat in the car, since Myra wasn't willing to stop long enough to eat. "Do you want me to drive?" she asked.

"No, I'm good. I'll let you know."

Trusting Cindy's word, she picked up her phone. Debated. Opened the messaging.

Are you okay?

She waited.

Finally, the answer flashed onto her screen.

Better, the closer we get.

Shit, did he feel as if he was being forced into this? That they had to be together to relieve the horrible ache they were both feeling?

The phone flashed again. *What's wrong?*

How to answer? If she said nothing, he would know she was lying. She didn't want to lie to him, but she didn't think texting was going to work.

I'm just worried about you.

The little graphic showed he was typing, but then that disappeared. Nothing happened. Then it showed typing again, and finally the message popped up.

Stop it.

She had to laugh so she did, and very carefully allowed a little bit of it to seep down their link.

Yes, sir.

Good girl.

She snorted.

"Hey, no sexting while I'm driving," Cindy called out.

She flashed her friend a smile. "No sexting, I promise."

They drove on for a couple of hours more before Cindy angled for an off-ramp. Myra felt that Adam was getting closer and closer, but he wasn't close enough yet. "Bathroom break?" she asked.

"No, I checked while you were in the shower. According to my calculations, this will be the best place to find a hotel to wait for him. Well, probably a motel."

It felt wrong to stop moving forward, but she had to appreciate Cindy's attention to detail. They scanned the limited options as they drove through town, Cindy abruptly turning into a driveway. "This chain is pretty good," she said as she found a parking spot.

"Not exactly romantic," Cindy worried as she looked around.

"Nothing about us has been particularly romantic," she pointed out.

Her friend frowned. "I don't like that for you."

Appreciating the love, Myra gave her a hug. "I need to tell him where we are." She was starting to feel anxious, both from the lack of forward movement and the feeling that he was getting closer and closer.

"God. This is awful. I've laughed at wolves in this state."

"No," Cindy said firmly. "You have not. They weren't in *this* state, and you know it. A bit of teasing when two wolves are on the verge of mating is one thing, this is totally different."

"You're right, you're right." She jumped up, paced. "I would have made a terrible drug addict," she laughed, hugging herself.

"I'm so sorry you're going through it this way. You deserve for it to have been perfect."

"I've had the perfect meet-and-mate. It was great, I'm not going to lie. But it was different. I didn't know Eric. God, I was scared then. I'd forgotten that."

"Scared?"

"Yeah. I mean, he was a stranger, I had no idea if he would like me. I felt so young and foolish."

"Psh, you were never young and foolish."

She laughed. "Sure I was. I wouldn't have been a very good teenager if I hadn't been."

"Okay, fair point. It's hard to picture you being anything but self-confident and in control."

She could only imagine that the look on her face was pure incredulity. Cindy burst out laughing at it, then conceded. "Okay, right now you're not so alpha as you usually are."

"Ha, you make me sound awful!"

"No, you're ours, and we love you. If you have any imperfections, they must fit right in, because we don't notice them."

"Crap, Cindy. Do you think I'm doing the right thing? Leaving?"

"That's not what I meant, and you would know it if you weren't so wound up. St. Louis needed you, but now you're needed elsewhere. I think, actually, now that this is happening..."

She paused, gave Myra a searching look, apparently liked what she saw. Myra held her breath.

"I think, what this means is that it's better for you and Adam to start together. It wouldn't have been the same for him, coming into your pack."

Myra frowned. "It happens all the time."

"Sure it does. But it's not Adam all the time. Maybe this is what he needed."

The rightness to that statement made her knees week and Myra sat back down on the bed. "Wow." She looked at Cindy and smiled. "I'm so glad I have you."

"Right back atcha."

She didn't stay down for long, too jittery. When her phone beeped, she jumped.

Meet me downstairs.

Close, he was so close.

"He wants me to meet him downstairs," she told Myra, heading for the door. Another beep. "Argh! He wants me to bring my bag. Where the heck does he think we're going to go?"

"You'll be fine, you'll be together, that's what matters."

"Yeah, sure. I don't believe you, but okay."

Cindy smothered a laugh, but she didn't fool Myra. They grabbed their things and headed out the door. By the time they'd reached the parking lot, Hillary's car was pulling in. Her friend jumped out, gave Myra a fierce hug, then shoved her into the car. She practically dove into Adam's lap, so grateful that he was welcoming her to him, pulling her in harder, kissing her deeply.

She was crying again, damn it, but she was so happy, and so horny and so relieved and still a bit nervous that somehow it would all go wrong. He moved her back over to the passenger seat and pulled her seat belt around, clicked it closed.

"We need to go," he said, his hand holding hers tightly. "It's not far, but I need you out of this car."

"Adam, we have a room, right here."

"Not good enough."

"But where are we going?"

"Don't worry, I've got it handled."

"You've never even been here!"

"Baby. This is still Hillary's territory. She knows people out here. I promise you, I've got us covered. Trust me."

Everything within her, except the raging need for him, stilled. Relaxed. "Okay."

They drove for ten minutes before he exited the highway again, following prompts from his phone. He squeezed her hand tightly enough that it might have gone numb, but she didn't care, didn't want him to relax the hold a smidge.

The area was sparsely populated, no houses very close to another. They turned down one lane, then another, then what she assumed was a driveway. She was proved correct only a minute later when they drove up to a pretty little house, its lights on in cheerful welcome. Damn, were they going to have to deal with people?

Adam grabbed her bag and she noticed he didn't have one, but didn't care enough to question. She just wanted to get him inside and alone. He walked up to the door and straight inside, smiling when she gave him a questioning look. "Just us."

He took her hand and led her down the hall to an open doorway. Candles lit the room, fresh flowers graced the dresser and rose petals were scattered on the duvet. A bottle of champagne and two glasses were on the bedside table.

"Oh," she sobbed, and ran for the bathroom to get a handful of tissues. She blew her nose and walked back into the room to find him leaning against the door.

"Not exactly the reaction I was expecting, but I'll take it."

His grin was sinful, and suddenly the urge to cry was gone. He seemed to notice and took two steps toward her. Stopped. "Myra, are you—" He shook his head, his face uncertain.

"What?"

"Are you holding yourself back from me? I love you, I should have said that before. Not even just before this." He waved at the air as if that explained the need to complete the mate bond. "But before you left Mountain View. I'm sorry for that, sorry that you think I'm here just because of this, but I promise you, if you give me a chance, I will make it right."

Stunned, she just stared at him. And then she understood. She'd been holding herself so tightly, so afraid to let her feelings flow down to him, and he could feel it. Feel that she was holding back.

She took a deep breath. Walked up to him and cupped his face in her hands. He mirrored her, his look so intent, so full of love and need for her. She let go.

And they burned, the heat exploding over them so hot, so fast, that she had his pants around his ankles before she considered his boots while he'd simply torn her shirt right off her back.

They each pulled apart to deal with their shoes and pants and then came together in a tangle of hands and legs, edging toward the bed until they fell on top of it, and each other.

CHAPTER ELEVEN

Adam tried to tell himself to slow down. To give her the romance she so deserved. But she was too busy attacking him for that to happen. Her fingers were twisted into his hair, her hand groping for his dick. He rolled them over until they were safely in the middle of the bed, landing so that she was on top of him. She drew in a sharp breath, then braced her hands on his shoulders and sat up, her gaze intent on his.

Then she smiled. It held such wicked delight that he knew he would never, ever regret the decision he'd made. He was a lucky, lucky bastard. She slid her hands down his chest, scratching lightly with her blunt nails. He put his hands on her hips and squeezed, then ran them up her sides to her breasts, cupped them firmly.

She leaned into his grip, brought a finger to his lips, slid it inside when he opened for her. He massaged her tits and swirled his tongue around her finger until she pulled it free and moved it to her clit.

"I could have done that for you, you know," he chided.

"Your hands are well occupied," she reminded him.

"Hm, so they are." He took both nipples with his fingers and pulled until she gasped. She circled her clit with her wet finger. His dick was rock hard now but trapped underneath her. He let her nipples free and gripped her ass, lifted. She helped him, reaching down for his cock, rubbing it in her juices before settling back down.

"Fuck."

She rubbed her slickness over him and he loved the feel of her wet fingers on him, but he couldn't wait any longer. "I need to be inside you."

"Yes," she agreed, rising up on her knees, placing him at her entrance. He held her still for a second, then together they lowered her onto him, his hips bucking up to meet her hard, and fast.

He felt it. Hadn't realized he would. Hadn't considered it. But he actually felt her soul twine with his. The beauty of it was so amazing he stopped moving, his hands on her hips holding her steady. She watched him, more hated tears dripping from her eyes, but he didn't care. He saw love and acceptance and the sparkle of heat that showed him she was right there with him. All the way.

"Wow," he breathed.

Her grin was huge. "Yeah." She dropped down, elbows going to either side of his face so she could kiss him. He wouldn't have thought their kisses could get better, but they did. Wrapping one arm tight across her back and twining his other hand through her hair, he began to move, even as they kissed. Pressing up into her, pushing her down onto him, over and over until the need overwhelmed him. He pulled free from the kiss and found the spot on her nape that still bore the faint mark from his teeth. He licked it and she quivered. He bit. They both shouted, the orgasms slamming through them as well as the solidification of their connection. She settled into his soul.

Myra sighed and went limp on top of him. He just held her tight and soaked in the feeling of them together.

As they slept, he never had to reach for her because she was always there. Ready for him. Eager for him. He wasn't even sure if the need was his, or hers, or just theirs. It didn't matter, each time they came together it was exactly what he needed, no matter if it was rough and fast or slow and sweet or a hilarious combination of the two. Each time, it was just them.

When dusk began to fall, he wrapped her in a blanket and led her out the back door to sit on the porch step. She sat between his knees, his chin on her shoulder, the blanket snug around them both, and they watched the stars come out.

"This," she said. "Always."

"Yes."

When they went inside, he led her to the kitchen, sat her down and while the coffee brewed, he pulled out the fresh fruit and croissants he'd asked for. There was jam and orange juice, which he hadn't thought to ask for, but appreciated. He set it all out on the table, then decided sitting on someone else's chair while naked wasn't exactly polite. They went upstairs and he pulled on his jeans, since that was all he had, while she slipped on a dress.

She broke open a croissant and spread the jelly on it, watching him as he sipped his coffee and decided what fruit he wanted to start with.

"I know, inside, that you're okay. Good. Great, even," she said. "But I still feel like I need to ask."

"Great works, if you want to downplay it a bit."

She smiled. "No worries?"

"No. I feel strong. Stronger. I definitely do not feel out of control."

"But you did, and I'm sorry for that."

"A taste of fear now and again is probably good for those as strong as we are. Keep our egos in check and help us remember that not everyone walks through life feeling as in control of themselves as we do."

She blinked at him.

He laughed. "I can do smart and introspective."

She threw a bit of bread at him. He caught it and ate it, then reached for her hand. "Seriously. I'm good. I had some time on the drive up to take a look at a map, picked a couple of cities in Arizona and New Mexico that I think we should check out."

"You know, we don't need to go there."

"I know. But I like the idea of laying those demons to rest and starting somewhere fresh together."

"Okay. Then that's what we'll do."

They talked and dreamed and wondered and planned, and after a while, he made her fried chicken for dinner.

EXCERPT

Going Deeper

(Wolf Appeal Book 3)

By KB Alan

(Available 3/11/19)

The opportunity to be one of the first members of a brand new werewolf pack is an exciting adventure for lifestyle blogger Cindy McCarthy. With her best friend by her side, she's ready for anything.

Jonas visits New Mexico to see this brand new pack in action and make sure it's a good home for his parents to retire to. Instead, he finds Cindy, and suddenly the visit takes on a whole new purpose. He's almost certain she's his mate, meant to be his forever.

Opening their souls to each other is only the beginning. They'll need to navigate setting up a new life together, with a new pack. One that has old dramas to put to bed and new relationships to forge. If Alicante can come together as a pack—a family—they all might survive the adventure intact.

CHAPTER ONE

Holding her breath, Cindy eased open the oven door and peeked inside. Then let the door drop with a thud when she saw what was waiting for her. It was her second attempt at making the apple bread recipe, and the second failure.

Grabbing the potholders that matched her pretty lemon-printed apron, she pulled the loaf pan out of the oven and set it on the counter. The "loaf" looked like an incredibly soggy pile of brown... well, it looked highly unappetizing.

Ah well, it was time to declare the recipe a failure. The question was, should she inform the company that had sent it to her—asking her to feature it on her blog—that she wasn't going to be able to accommodate them, or post the recipe, showing pictures of the failed results, asking her readers to do their own tests and report back with outcome? Decisions, decisions.

She was glad she'd tried the recipe now, in her familiar oven. If it had failed in her new oven, once she moved, she'd have wondered if the appliance was to blame.

Grabbing her camera, she took several shots of the mess, just in case. She wasn't against posting failures, sometimes they were appreciated by her readers, but she preferred to be able to end the post with success, or be able to identify what she thought was wrong with the recipe. Well, she'd give it some thought, but had the pictures recorded if she needed them.

Leaving the pan to cool before she attempted cleaning it out, she hung up her apron and went to her office. While the kitchen looked spotless and beautiful, in her ever-so-humble opinion, the office looked like a disaster, with moving boxes piled high and her desk empty of everything except the computer and printer. The bookshelves were all packed up, and she'd decided to work on the linen closet next. She put the camera on the empty bookshelf and grabbed the tape gun and large marker.

When the phone in her pocket rang with her mother's ringtone, she tried not to grimace. And failed. She plucked her earbuds out of her pocket and plugged them in before pressing the button to accept the call. No way was this going to be a short conversation.

"Hi, Mom."

"Cynthia, how come I had to hear from your aunt Laura that you've rented your house out?"

"I told you I decided to rent it out instead of selling it."

"Yes, but not that you'd found someone."

"It's a nice house in a good location, especially for another pack member. I told you I didn't think it would take long to find someone."

Her mother ignored that reminder. "I'm still not convinced this is a good idea."

"Flying to see you in Texas won't be much different if I'm coming from Arizona than when I come from St. Louis."

"I know, it's not that. But what can Myra be thinking, leaving her pack? They love her, and I thought she loved being alpha of St. Louis. An alpha can't just up and leave her pack on a whim, it's not natural."

"If her mate had been anyone else, certainly another alpha, one of them would have had to leave their pack, and you wouldn't have thought anything of it."

"I don't think I trust this Adam character," Dana said, switching tacks.

Cindy bit her tongue, figuratively, and counted to five. "You haven't even met him."

"It's not right that he's been in hiding all these years. What does he have to hide? A strong alpha, a good one, should have been part of a pack."

"Mom. You know he was turned against his will. Why would he then jump right into pack life with a bunch of werewolves, after being viciously attacked by them?"

"That rogue pack was not normal and you know it." The indignation in her mother's voice was clear and had Cindy rolling her eyes as she taped the bottom of a box closed and flipped it over. She took it to the linen closet and studied the contents.

"I do know it. It was crazy and I still can't believe it happened, but it did. But he had no way of knowing that, so why would you be surprised that he stayed away from anything werewolf until he found out otherwise?"

"If he's smart, it shouldn't have taken him so long."

Cindy sighed. "Mom, when you heard that Zach out in Mountain View had found his mate the same way, finding Hillary, who'd been avoiding wolves since she was attacked by those same crazy people, you didn't mistrust *her*. You were sympathetic and worried about her."

"It's not the same."

"Why? I think you're being sexist."

Her mother sputtered, but Cindy thought she was on to something. "You hold Adam to a different standard than you did Hillary. If Myra hadn't decided to leave St. Louis, Adam would be coming here to be my alpha anyway. So what's the difference if I choose to go to Arizona, and they are too, and so they're my alphas there instead of here?" She was genuinely confused about her mother's problem.

Dana sighed. "It's time you came back home to Texas. There's no reason to move to another state again."

"Ah." She put the box down and flopped onto the couch. That was so not happening. Ever. And she was shocked her mother wanted it to happen.

"It's embarrassing that you make like our pack's not good enough for you."

Cindy tried, in vain, to formulate a response to that ridiculous statement, but her mother forged on.

"You know that Brenda wouldn't be a problem if you came back home, right? Whatever issues you girls had in the past, I'm sure you could—"

"Mom," Cindy interrupted. "It's not about Brenda. I like the idea of helping to build a new pack from scratch. I don't know that I'll ever go back to Texas."

When she'd moved eighteen years ago, it hadn't been because of her old boss, Brenda, though she supposed her mom would see it that way. Her first job out of college hadn't gone well, mostly because she'd lost respect for her boss, who happened to be the fourth in her pack's hierarchy. The respect issue had been about Brenda's business decisions, but she couldn't deny that it carried over into her respect of the woman as a pack leader.

The hierarchy was the pack leadership, with the pack alpha at the top—two, if they were mated—and then the first, second, third and fourth, down from there. The ranking was based purely on power, with each wolf or mated pair taking different responsibilities in the running of the pack. If Cindy had chosen to stay, it would have been a bit of effort to not let that lack of respect show amongst the pack, but she could have done it.

"Really, I didn't leave because of Brenda. I told you, once I started looking for another job, I realized that the whole country was available to me, and I liked the idea of trying out somewhere new." She had, in fact, told her parents that several times.

"You didn't even keep the job in St. Louis for very long before quitting," Dana said, as if that meant the choice to move there had been a mistake.

"No, because the blog took off in a way I never could have foreseen. It gave me an interesting challenge for a long time, but now it runs so smoothly, I think changing things up again will be good for me. Call it my midlife crises if you want."

"Cynthia, you're only forty-one."

"The perfect age to try something new. It's not like there's a risk to it, Mom. My job is very stable and successful and I can do it from anywhere in the country. Heck, I could go to Europe if I wanted to."

"You need to stop gallivanting around and find your mate."

Cindy sighed, but not audibly. How in the world her mother could sound insulted over this conversation was beyond Cindy. And wasn't gallivanting around going to make her more likely to find her mate than staying home, where she already knew her mate *wasn't*?

Having no idea how to respond, she just waited.

"It's not too late to have children, you know."

This time, she let the sigh be audible. "I don't have a whole lot of control with the whole finding-my-mate thing, Mom. You can't blame me for that one. And traveling around, meeting more packs, that will help with my chances, don't you think?"

Werewolves knew pretty quickly when they'd met their mates. They could have relationships before that, but they usually didn't last long, as both parties knew it wasn't the real thing. She'd enjoyed several relationships, but none longer than eight months. And it was very rare for a werewolf to get pregnant from anyone other than their mate, so even her mother couldn't blame her for not producing grandchildren.

"That's true." Apparently this was a new idea to her mom, because Dana's voice brightened at the idea. "You said you were going to help Myra interview some of the wolves who wanted to join the new pack?"

"That's right." Myra, her best friend for sixteen years, was her current alpha. She'd been the one to shut down the Mesa Pack when Hillary had mated Zach, and it had been discovered that there was a rogue pack doing horrific things out in Arizona. It had been Myra's job as the National President, elected to serve a one-year term as the head werewolf in the United States, to determine the fates of every member of both packs. She'd had to condemn to death the wolves who had been actively involved in abducting, attacking and murdering people in the supposed effort to turn them into werewolves. Since that wasn't how werewolves were turned, it wasn't a surprise to any sane wolf that the process hadn't worked most of the time, and only two people had survived—Hillary and Adam—several years apart.

Cindy couldn't imagine sentencing anyone to death, but then again, her friend was the alpha for a reason. Personally, Cindy was happy to be a typical werewolf, not part of the hierarchy, let alone an alpha. The idea of choosing who would die versus who would be sent to other packs seriously made her nauseous. But Myra had handled it, finding homes for those who weren't to die, working with the pack alphas across the country to determine the best situation for every one of the wolves.

Then she'd gone on a search for Adam, knowing only that a single wolf besides Hillary had survived being attacked by the rogue pack, and wanting to find him and ensure that he was living a safe and healthy life.

Cindy would never forget the moment her best friend discovered that the man was her mate. She shivered at the thought of that level of emotion ever going through her. Although maybe it wouldn't be as extreme, since alphas were generally hit by the magic of the mate bond more strongly than the average wolf.

"You'll come visit when we get settled," she invited. Her parents had only visited St. Louis once in all the years she'd been there, so she felt fairly safe in issuing the invitation. "We're just going to rent for a while, make sure the area we choose is a good selection for the whole pack. There are a lot of things to consider, and we may not find the right town the first go."

"All right, I guess that will do. I'll let you get to your packing and tell your father you said hello."

"Thanks, Mom. And give my love to Bill, Juanita, and the kids when you see them." Her brother and his wife were frequent visitors to her parents' house, a fact that amazed her. She swore it was like she and her brother had completely different parents. For sure, they had completely different relationships with them.

She hung up and switched the phone to music, then went at the linen closet with renewed vigor. Maybe she couldn't articulate exactly why this move felt like the right thing, but she was certain that it was. She'd been very seriously considering the idea even before she'd mentioned it to Myra and discovered that her best friend was thinking the same thing. That had just solidified it for them both, and nothing since had led her to question the decision.

Meeting Adam, shortly after he and Myra had mated, made it clear how right the decision had been. She'd instantly felt comfortable with him, and looked forward to him being her alpha and to helping him understand that he was meant to be a leader of wolves, not a loner.

After the linen closet, she tackled the guest bathroom. She had some friends coming over tomorrow to help with the kitchen and move the boxes into the container she'd rented, one that would be transported to their destination when she was ready. In the meantime, they just needed to explore a couple of cities and make a decision on where to begin.

Jonas groaned when the phone rang with his mother's ringtone. He loved his mother, but she refused to acknowledge that his current job as a bartender, almost always covering the closing shift, should influence what time she decided to chat. The fact that he was in a time zone three hours behind hers also seemed to make little impact.

He accepted the call and brought the phone to his ear, flinging his other arm over his eyes. He kept meaning to get better drapes, but...well, who really wanted to go drapery shopping? Not him.

"Hi, Mom."

"Jonas, is it really necessary to grumble at me like that when I call?"

"Only when you call at seven-thirty, and I didn't go to bed until three."

"It's ridiculous that you have a job that keeps you out until three in the morning. But it's hardly my fault."

He wasn't going to go there. While his parents weren't actively against his move to a slower-paced life three years ago, neither were they impressed with his decision to take a job they considered beneath him. They seemed to have missed that the whole point in selling his business as a high-end recruiter in New York City was to try life at a more relaxed pace.

Joining the Mountain View pack, in Idaho, had been the right choice. And the job at the pack's bar—one they worked to keep wolf only, no humans—was perfect. He had little to no stress and enjoyed interacting with his fellow pack members. It had been a great way to get to know them better. Though they were a friendly enough bunch, they didn't get a lot of new members who weren't mates, so his wandering in and becoming part of the group had been greatly helped by accepting the job as bartender.

Since he had chosen not to respond, his mother apparently decided to move on.

"Your father and I are thinking of moving."

"What?" They'd been in their house since before he'd been born. "Is there a problem or something? You know if you need help..."

Her voice softened at his offer. "No problem, it's just like you said, time to consider a new pace in life. We've been in the city forever but it's not such a great place to retire, we're thinking."

"Wait. You're not just moving houses, but out of the city? Where are you thinking?"

"Arizona."

"What?" This time it was more of a shout than a question. He dropped his arm from his face and sat up so fast, his head swam a bit. His parents had always lived in New York. *Their* parents had always lived in New York. They'd acted like he was crazy when he'd said he was leaving.

"We think the dry air would be good for your father's arthritis. Besides, it's exciting, this new pack. Myra Talmidge was out your way, did you meet her? What did you think?"

He blinked at the unexpected change of direction that he should have seen coming. "No, I didn't meet her. I did meet her mate, Adam. Played a game of pool with him but he was starting a bit of a mating frenzy, from being separated from Myra, so I don't suppose it's a good experience to judge him on. Still, I'd say he's probably a good guy. No experience being alpha, but it's in him, no question. He's strong."

"That's good to know. We emailed Myra and we'll see what happens. I'm sure she'll want some experienced elders in her pack." Her voice was a bit uncertain.

"I think you're probably right, Mom, I just want to make sure it's the right decision for you. You've never talked about leaving New York."

"We are getting older, you know. And while I still think it's a bit ridiculous that you retired at your age, at our age it's acceptable."

He let the dig go, not interested in rehashing a decision that had already been made, and had turned out to be an excellent one, in his opinion.

"We want to try it out, while we're young enough to enjoy the change. Plus, if we decide we hate living somewhere without snow, we can always come back."

"True. Listen, Myra's become good friends with Zach and Larry. Why don't you let me get in touch with her, have a chat, see what they're thinking with all this."

"Honey, I don't think you should call your alpha that name."

He just laughed. "You'll have to meet her sometime, Mom. In the meantime, let me have a chat with Myra or Adam, or both of them, and feel things out a bit."

"That would be nice, Jonas. Thank you."

"You bet. I'll let you know what I find out."

He disconnected and let the idea simmer a bit. It actually wasn't a bad one. In their early seventies, it was true his parents should start thinking about where they wanted to live out their retirement, and somewhere without the bother of snow would be good. Although there were always younger pack members ready to make a buck shoveling out the elders' driveways, his parents liked their independence, and he could see how they might appreciate not having to rely on others for tasks they'd handled their whole lives.

Rolling off the bed, he scratched and stretched and reached for the sweatpants hanging off the end of the mattress, pulling them on. There was no way he was getting back to sleep, so he might as well roll with it. Besides, he had the day off.

He quickly poached a couple of eggs and decided to head out to the pack house, see who was around for a run. If he was lucky, since it was the weekend, one of his alphas would be there and he could ask their opinion on the matter. If not, he'd track them down later and take the time to let the idea work in his brain.

The pack house was alive with the wolves who lived there as well as several other pack members like himself, who were interested in a group run. Zach, in wolf form, was playing with a group of adolescents on the grass, and Jonas had to smile at their antics. He went into the house and found a spot for his clothes, then made the shift. He ran into Stephen, their second, on his way off the porch, and they raced into the woods together. The other man beat him in the long run, but it was a good chase.

He enjoyed this adopted pack, had made several friends, but he did need to start considering a permanent situation. He liked his job, but he'd taken it on as a favor to fill a vacant slot. Was it what he wanted to do for the foreseeable future? Maybe, maybe not. He was renting a small apartment that he'd found when he'd first hit town three years ago, and had intended to stay in only shortly, while he got a feel for the place. Inertia had kept him there, but maybe he should consider finding a more permanent home.

Not entirely sure how he'd gone from contemplating his parents' future to his own, he took a short nap in the sun with several of his packmates, at home with the group, and yet suddenly not certain he was really home.

To join KB Alan's newsletter and be informed of new releases, sign up at kbalan.com/newsletter

Find more about Going Deeper at kbalan.com/books/going-deeper

ALSO BY KB ALAN

Perfect Fit Series

Perfect Formation (Book 1)

Perfect Alignment (Book 2)

Perfect Stranger (Book 2.5)

Perfect Addition (Book 3)

Wolf Appeal Series

Alpha Turned (Book 1)

Challenge Accepted (Book 2)

Going Deeper (Book 3)

Fully Invested (Contemporary Romance)

(Part of the Wildlife Ridge World)

Coming Home (Book 1)

Breaking Free (Book 2)

Stand Alone

Bound by Sunlight

Keeping Claire

Sweetest Seduction

kbalan.com

ABOUT THE AUTHOR

KB Alan lives the single life in Southern California. She acknowledges that she should probably turn off the computer and leave the house once in a while in order to find her own happily ever after, but for now she's content to delude herself with the theory that Mr. Right is bound to come knocking at her door through no real effort of her own. Please refrain from pointing out the many flaws in this system. Other comments, however, are happily received.

Visit her website at www.kbalan.com.

To be join her newsletter and be informed of new releases, sign up at kbalan.com/newsletter.

Made in the USA
Monee, IL
15 March 2021

62806516R00105